MW01633965

JENNA'S SEAL (SPECIAL FORCES: OPERATION ALPHA)

FINDING HOME, BOOK 1

JULIA BRIGHT

This book is a work of fiction. Names, characters, places, and incidents are products of the author's imagination or used fictitiously. Any resemblance to actual events or locales or persons living or dead is entirely coincidental.

© 2021 ACES PRESS, LLC. ALL RIGHTS RESERVED

No part of this work may be used, stored, reproduced or transmitted without written permission from the publisher except for brief quotations for review purposes as permitted by law.
This book is licensed for your personal enjoyment only. This book may not be re-sold or given away to other people. If you would like to share this book with another person, please purchase an additional copy for each recipient. If you're reading this book and did not purchase it, or it was not purchased for your use only, please purchase your own copy.

Dear Readers,

Welcome to the Special Forces: Operation Alpha Fan-Fiction world!

If you are new to this amazing world, in a nutshell the author wrote a story using one or more of my characters in it. Sometimes that character has a major role in the story, and other times they are only mentioned briefly. This is perfectly legal and allowable because they are going through Aces Press to publish the story.

This book is entirely the work of the author who wrote it. While I might have assisted with brainstorming and other ideas about which of my characters to use, I didn't have any part in the process or writing or editing the story.

I'm proud and excited that so many authors loved my characters enough that they wanted to write them into their own story. Thank you for supporting them, and me!

READ ON!
Xoxo
Susan Stoker

CHAPTER 1

Jenna Mettler stared up at the barrel of the shotgun, fear holding her still. The boy pointing the gun at her couldn't have been over fifteen, maybe as young as thirteen. She hadn't asked his age when he'd rushed in with the other men, taking them captive.

The last thing she wanted to do was to die at the hands of a petrified teenager. He had to be frightened based on how his hands shook. His eyes were wide as saucers, and his lips pulled back as though he couldn't get enough air in his lungs. His chest rose and fell rapidly like he'd been chasing someone on a football field and stopped to take a breath. But this kid wasn't playing games. He was here to kill.

She'd taken this assignment as one last hurrah, even if it would be an extended hurrah. Right for the part with all the right assets to get the senator's attention, she'd signed up to become an assistant, traveling with him, researching for him, and while he wasn't looking, digging through his files to find information on him.

Devlin loved having a pretty aide on his team, and her handlers at the CIA had told her she was the perfect agent to get the job. She'd told them she was too old at thirty-one, that he'd probably go for someone closer to twenty, but she'd been wrong. Now that she was here in Turkey, lying on her back in a hunting cabin that erred on the side of glamping, she wished she would have left the agency instead of agreed to one final assignment.

Her body jerked when someone on the other end of the camp fired off a round. The boy pulled the gun closer to his body, his eyes growing wider. Fright passed over his features, making her wonder how willing he was to be here in this role of possible executioner. Had they conscripted him, forcing him to be a soldier when all he wanted to do was stay in school and play ball with his friends? She doubted he would understand if she spoke to him. Maybe he knew English, maybe not.

Jenna bit her cheek, praying they could get out of this. Someone shouted outside, and the kid turned away from her and Dani. He moved to the door and opened it.

"What should we do?" Dani whispered as she leaned in close.

Jenna shrugged, acting like she had no clue what to do in a situation like this. They weren't alone yet, so she said nothing. She didn't want this kid's attention or the attention of anyone else in their raiding party. If she got a chance to act, she would.

Relief slipped through Jenna as the boy stepped outside, leaving them alone. She waited for a beat before she pulled her cellphone from her back pocket and typed in a phone number she had memorized. She should have already sent a message, but their captors had surprised her while she'd been asleep.

"Is your phone working?" Dani asked.

Jenna glanced at the door, then back to Dani. "I'm not sure." She typed in a short message, knowing it may very well be ignored. She turned away from Dani, hiding her typing as she explained as much as she could and hoped the man she sent the message to didn't ignore her.

"Should we look and see what they're doing?" Dani asked.

Jenna shook her head as she shoved her phone

into her pocket after she hit send. Only a few minutes had passed, and there wasn't any reason to believe they'd left the camp. The kid was probably right outside.

"No, don't move. I'll go look," Jenna said.

Dani scoffed. "Please, Leanne, I've had more training than you. Do you have a death wish? This is actually dangerous, not at all like your cushy job as my husband's aide."

Both Senator Devlin and his wife, Dani, believed she had never been in the military or had any training in close combat skills. They also thought her name was Leanne Armstrong, and they certainly had no clue she was in the CIA and had spent the last few years on a dangerous assignment in Tunisia.

Jenna didn't have a death wish. She just knew what to look for and how to avoid being seen. Dani had been in the national guard for three years. She hadn't received any specialized training, other than the basics of how to shoot a gun and run ten miles with a pack on her back. She wasn't a spy and had little to no training in surveillance.

If Jenna spoke up, she would blow her cover. That was the last thing she wanted to do because she still didn't know how dirty Senator Devlin's latest schemes were. Jenna nodded, letting Dani think she was still the same woman who'd come to work for Devlin at one of his friend's suggestions. Though Jenna didn't dislike Dani, she didn't trust her. She didn't doubt that Dani would tell her husband everything, even if she said she would keep things in confidence.

At least Jenna had sent the text to Admiral Light. Maybe it would be answered, perhaps it wouldn't. Few knew she worked for the CIA, and even fewer knew she worked for Senator Devlin. Her job with Devlin was behind the scenes and she was working under a fake name. She had no family who would miss her. The CIA wouldn't come looking for her, but they might look for Devlin.

She would have to keep her image out of the media if they were rescued. Not that many would recognize her with her salon-created red hair and contacts that turned her brown eyes blue. In her previous assignment, her naturally blonde hair had been turned dark brown. After she finished working for Devlin, she would go back to blonde if she wasn't gray by now. She'd been through enough stress that she might just be all gray with only a few strands of blonde.

She didn't need eye correction, so she wouldn't go back to wearing glasses. It had been years since she'd been herself. Did she even know who she was without the CIA? She hoped she survived this so she could live as Jenna Mettler and not some random CIA agent who could die and no one would ever know.

Devlin would be pissed if he figured out she was a CIA agent. He would probably open a can of worms that would spill over the CIA, tarnishing the agency. But Devlin was selling state secrets and had already gotten five hundred American military personnel killed when critical information had been given to a terrorist organization. The intelligence the CIA had gathered pointed directly at Devlin. Somehow, he'd deflected the blame, though it rested solely with him. Now she was trying to block his next action and save lives. It would be nice to take him down but stopping his terrorist acts was her primary focus.

Another volley of gunfire erupted, and the door to the cabin flew open. Dani jerked back as the man who opened the door let his hand fly, slapping her across the face.

Jenna jumped forward and caught Dani, keeping her from hitting the ground. The jolt of Dani falling had pushed Jenna to the floor. She stared up at the man who had just barged in. It wasn't the kid with the gun. Instead, this man looked like he knew what he was doing, and fear played no part in his actions.

"You will come with me. No talking either," the guy barked.

Jenna's only hope was the text she'd sent to her father's old friend. She'd given their location, the situation, and her new name. Hopefully, he would be able to react.

Admiral Light had served under her father a long time ago. She'd met Light when she'd been a child. As an adult, she'd been able to meet with Admiral Light a few times, and they'd gone to dinner at least once. Of course, her being a Marine had been a point of jokes with him, but he'd said he'd been proud of her when she'd joined up.

His attitude changed significantly the day she quit the military. He'd called her and asked her why. She couldn't tell him she'd been approached by the CIA. The military hadn't been her long-term plan. She'd joined to serve her country, but she'd never believed she would be a career woman, retiring from the Marines at a ripe old age like her father had from the Navy. Too bad he'd not lived to enjoy his retirement.

She'd always assumed she would leave the military and begin working for some company. But the job with the CIA had intrigued her, promising her more freedom to cut terrorists down and make the world safer.

By the time she'd been born, her father had been in the Navy for more than twenty years. He'd risen in the ranks and had command of a ship. The long months away had damaged his relationship with her mother. Of course, her father had kids with another woman who he'd married when they were both eighteen. Military life hadn't been for his first wife, either.

Jenna hardly talked to her half-siblings. They honestly hated her, which, as an adult, she understood in a way. As a kid, she'd thought they were mean. Now she wondered if she would ever have time to clear the air with them. They hadn't been at fault, and neither had she. If anything, it was their father who hadn't been able to handle life in the military with a family.

"Get in there." The man pointed his gun toward the main cabin where Senator Devlin had been staying. The only reason Dani had been in Jenna's cabin was another party had joined them. Strangers, actually, but Devlin made fast friends with one of the men, and they'd demanded the women leave. She wasn't sure if Birch had stayed or not, but he hadn't entered her cabin. And where was Andrew? Had he been with the senator last night? She didn't trust Andrew at all, but Birch wasn't too bad of a guy.

It seemed rather convenient and not in a good way that Devlin had bonded so fast with the strangers. That they'd eaten alone last night had thrown off all sorts of red flags. Jenna had tried to go out for a walk at one point, but a guard at the door insisted she stay with Dani, claiming the area to be too dangerous for a nighttime stroll. When she'd tried to sneak out through a window, she'd learned they'd been screwed shut. Another guard had been positioned at the back door. Now they were being held hostage, and she had no clue what had happened with Devlin, Andrew, Birch or the strangers. Were these men holding them an extension of the group Devlin had eaten dinner with? Or was this something else totally different?

The larger cabin had a full kitchen and a movie watching room along with multiple bedrooms. She was glad they weren't all crammed into the one cabin, but last night it would have been useful. She could have spied on Devlin. Instead, she'd been relegated to her room, forced to stay separate from Devlin.

Jenna stepped into the large cabin, quickly

taking in the situation. Devlin was sitting in a chair at the table, a laptop computer in front of him. His gaze lifted for half a second, then he went back to staring at the computer screen. Birch was seated at the opposite end of the table with Andrew across from him. He didn't seem happy. The stranger Devlin had dined with the night before wasn't around.

"You," a guy with a gun stepped closer to her and jerked his head toward the kitchen. "Cook us food."

She wasn't a great cook, but she would fake it. If it meant she had the freedom to move, maybe it would mean she could send another text or something. Her phone was stuffed in her pocket with her shirt untucked. They hadn't searched her, which seemed rather short-sighted, but she wasn't going to complain about their lack of attentiveness.

Jenna found chicken, vegetables, some pasta, and sauce. She started cutting vegetables as she contemplated what she could do with the kitchen knives. Four guys had guns. The kid with the gun wasn't inside, but he might still be around. She didn't know if more people were hanging out around the camp.

Her butt vibrated, and her eyes grew wide as she stared at the cutting board. She prayed the man in charge hadn't heard her vibrating phone. She didn't dare look up and find out if he was paying attention to her.

Could Admiral Light be close? She had no clue where he was in the world. She didn't know whether he was stateside or somewhere out in the middle of the ocean. They needed a miracle if they were going to survive. Maybe he knew of someone who was positioned near her. If something drastic didn't happen soon, they would be screwed.

After she cooked and served the meal, she was allowed to use the restroom. Still, no one checked her for a phone. Alone in the bathroom, she pulled out her phone and saw a reply. It was one word, and it brought a smile to her lips.

SEAL displayed large and in caps in her message application. She typed in one word for a reply, *YES*, then flushed the toilet to make it sound like she was doing something.

A knock sounded on the door, and she grunted. "I'm still going," she called out, hopefully making them think she needed more time. At least they'd allowed her to shut the door. They obviously didn't know she had a phone. If they found her with the device, they would have been pissed.

Jenna put the phone on do not disturb and then deleted the messages she'd sent to Admiral Light.

She prayed he didn't need to communicate with her because she had to hide the phone here. Later, she would try to recover the device and send more messages if required. Surely the admiral would understand if she didn't reply.

She stepped out of the bathroom and moved to the couch next to Dani. She hadn't gotten enough sleep the night before, and exhaustion ate at her. Dani yawned, too. They were probably all tired, but the men holding them didn't seem tired.

How long would this go on? The sun was already up above the trees, and it didn't seem like this group of terrorists or whatever they were was getting anywhere close to heading out. Would they have to spend another night like this?

Birch sat with his arms crossed over his chest, anger flashing in his eyes. Had something happened while she'd been in the bathroom? She glanced at Devlin and saw a panicked look on his face.

"This is wrong," Birch said.

"Watch it," Devlin spit out.

The guy in charge moved close. "What did you say?"

"There is no reason to hold us. Let us go. We don't even know who you are and this—" Birch was cut off as the man's hand flew fast, knocking him to the floor.

Jenna wanted to jump up and help him, but one of the men with guns watched her like a hawk. If she stood up, she would probably be shot.

The man grabbed Birch by the back of his shirt and dragged him over to the door, then outside with the help of one of the other men. Jenna turned to watch, angry she couldn't help. They would kill her if she moved.

The men forced Birch to stand then told him to run. Jenna bit her lip and closed her eyes just as a gun went off. A sob escaped her lips before she could force the anger and sadness down. Birch could be rude at times, and he was a jerk when it came to women, but he wasn't an awful person who deserved to die.

Dani let out a wail as tears streamed down her cheeks. The senator hardly looked moved. Andrew's eyes were wide open, and he looked a little feral. But he didn't move. Their captors had proven they didn't value life.

Was this deeper than surface appearance? Did Senator Devlin think Birch was a mole working for the CIA or another alphabet agency? Had her position been compromised? She needed more information, but it didn't seem like she was going to get it now. Not with Dani crying and their captors agitated.

She and Dani were led into a bedroom and told to stay put. She needed to rest, so she dropped to the bed and tried to sleep.

"What are you doing?" Dani asked.

"I can't do anything this tired. Get some sleep. Who knows what they will do next?"

The bed moved, and she felt Dani's arm brush up against her. "Do you think it will get worse?" Dani's voice shook with fear.

Jenna rolled over and met Dani's gaze. She wanted to tell Dani it was certainly going to get worse, but she didn't trust the woman. If Jenna revealed anything, Dani would report back to Devlin. "Sleep while you can. These people aren't here for fun."

Dani was right to worry. They could be dead by nightfall. Jenna prayed Admiral Light sent the guys fast. She knew from experience waiting for a rescue would take time. If no one was close, it might take a few days for a team to arrive. Hopefully, they would still be alive when and if the SEALs showed up.

CHAPTER 2

Jason "Vine" Chase made his way up to the bridge. He hadn't even finished his meal, but Admiral Light wouldn't have pulled him away from his food if it wasn't important. They'd just finished a mission in Georgia, the country not the state, and were headed out to the Mediterranean where they'd meet up with another ship and then hitch a ride on a helicopter to a base and finally a plane home to Hawaii.

He loved his job, loved the rush of the missions, and loved saving people. He didn't love the trip home. It would take more than a day to get to Hawaii, sometimes four days after missions, and if they were unlucky, they could be traveling or stalled for over a week. But the military told them where and when to go, and they went. It was part of being a SEAL.

He'd seen the world, that was for sure, and so far, he still liked his job. He enjoyed rescuing people from horrible situations. There were a few times he wished he had more sleep, but he could sleep on the plane or on a ship. Which was why they were eating at this hour and not with the rest of the crew. Messed up hours was just one of the perks of being a SEAL.

Vine stepped through the open door, looking for the admiral. The bridge wasn't a place he'd spent a lot of time on. Though a Navy man through and through, he wasn't ever going to work on a bridge, and he didn't want one. He knew this was what some aspired to, but all the instruments, being constantly under the eye of the highest-ranking Navy members, it was too much for him. He wanted space to think. Besides, his sarcasm slid out too easily. Up here, with the admiral or captain crawling all over him, he'd lose his shit and get tossed from the bridge to the brig in seconds.

Someone stepped out from behind a closed door to his right. He turned, saw the admiral, and saluted. His movement felt stiff, like he was forcing it. He didn't like the bridge at all. He would be more comfortable on a Zodiac storming a beach.

"At ease," Light said as he waved him into the room and closed the door behind them. "We have an issue. Normally, this isn't something we would jump on so fast, but—" Light blew out a heavy breath as he shook his head. "This is messed up. I've already spoken to the Pentagon, and we're going in. Since you're on my ship, your group was volunteered."

"Yes, sir. We're happy to do whatever is needed."

"That's good because this is sticky and bound to get messier."

Vine had no clue what was going on, but he didn't like the worried look on Admiral Light's face. From what Vine knew, Admiral Light was solid and didn't get ruffled. The man looked visibly upset. Light moved to a table with a map out.

"I received a text from a family friend. She's gotten herself into an interesting position. She's working on Senator Devlin's staff, and he and his wife, along with two other aides, were taken hostage. They are being held captive in this location." Light pointed to the map. "It's on the border of Georgia and Turkey near the water. We don't have any ground troupes near the camp, and it was determined your team could get there fastest."

Vine stared at the map, taking in the topography, knowing a raid in the area would be tricky. "Do we have any overhead surveillance?"

"Not yet. We're working on getting a satellite pointed in that direction. And I've lost contact with the person on the ground. Honestly, I wasn't expecting her to answer her phone. That she got a text off in the middle of this, I'm impressed. I need you to get your team ready. We've swung around, and you'll be close enough to head out in about thirty to forty-five minutes. I know you're tired, but—"

Vine held up his hand and cut off the admiral. "This is what we train to do." He was sure most naval officers or crew members wouldn't dare to interrupt an admiral. This was why he didn't want to work on a bridge, ever.

Light flashed him a smile. "I knew you'd be ready to dive in."

"Yes, sir. We'll be prepared. How many people are in Devlin's travel group?"

"Four or five. I think five, but we're not positive."

"Thank you, sir. We'll bring them home safely."

Admiral Light shifted from one foot to another. He looked uncomfortable, which was odd for an admiral. He cleared his throat, then met Vine's gaze. "The person who contacted me is a close family friend. She's important to me. Right now, she's working as Devlin's aide."

Vine nodded. "Why do I get the feeling there is more to this than you are saying?"

Light's lips twitched up. "You're perceptive. It's probably why you're a good SEAL. Don't lose that."

"Yes, sir."

"She seems to be working undercover."

"Undercover?" Vine didn't understand.

Light nodded. "Yes. She's going by Leanne. She's capable, but she may not be allowing Devlin to know how capable she is. Go tell your men to prepare. This is going to be dicey. We have no clue how many men are holding them, but she said they were separated into two cabins, so count on at least four, possibly more."

"Yes, sir."

"Thank you. I know it's your job but thank you for doing it."

Vine left the bridge and headed down to the mess to tell his team they had to go again. They'd slept for about six hours, and it would have to be enough. They may or may not be able to sleep in the next twenty-four. Whatever happened to the senator and his group, Vine would make sure the group who took them captive paid dearly.

The SEALs landed on the rocky shore about a mile from the camp. They each had their tasks and specialties. Since they didn't know what they were walking into, they'd brought a small amount of explosives along with their usual weapons.

"You ready?" Legs asked.

Legs hadn't gotten his name because he was a leg man, though he was. No, Legs had quads that wouldn't quit. Added to the fact his legs were long, the name stuck. Legs was amazingly acrobatic when it came to doing maneuvers up or down buildings, and he wasn't too bad on the ground either. Vine would be lying to say he wasn't jealous of how Legs could move.

Vine gave a quick nod. "I'm ready to blast these bastards to hell for taking the senator and his team."

"Yeah," Legs said. "I can't believe what they've been through. Minx is prepared to treat the injured. Hopefully, they'll be able to make it back to the zodiac."

Vine didn't know what he would do if the members of the senator's party couldn't walk.

Maybe they'd have to commandeer a vehicle. If they couldn't be moved, hopefully, the Navy would send in a helicopter.

Minx knew directions in the northern hemisphere, even without a compass. His father had insisted he understand the stars and how to get home, dropping him in the middle of fields and forests to test his abilities. Minx had survived and learned, using his knowledge no matter where they were. As long as they weren't in South America or Australia. Then he would need to study the stars before they let him loose in the wild.

Wig and Quirk followed up in the rear, and Astro kept his eye out for any strays trying to guard the camp. His team was about the best group of guys he knew. They could do things he'd never thought possible. Vine knew his own abilities, but these guys impressed the heck out of him.

Minx halted their movement, and Vine caught up with him. "What's up?"

Minx pointed to the left, and Vine followed the line, seeing two people walking a perimeter. He motioned for Quirk and Wig to move on them. They would go down and take out the pair.

The rest of the team hung back for a few seconds

while Quirk and Wig moved silently forward. He only heard a slight crunch when they took out the two guys. Anyone else would have thought it was an animal.

Next, they found and cleared the first cabin. Vine and Astro moved to the second cabin, clearing it. There were two other structures in the clearing. One of them was larger and probably housed the senator.

They were about fifteen feet from the main cabin when the door flew open. Two women were led out, one of them sobbing, the other looking so angry she could spit nails. They were taken to the cabin he and his team had just cleared.

Vine and Astro were closest. He met Astro's gaze and nodded. Working with these guys was great. They understood him. He didn't need to tell Astro what to do. The man had known where to go and how to approach based on Vine's hand movements.

The door opened, and one of the men stepped out. Astro was on him, taking the dude down as Vine slipped inside. It took him less than a second to see the two women sitting on the floor and a big guy about five feet away, his gun resting on the table behind him.

Vine didn't have time to waste and moved fast,

jerking the guy away from the gun. Before he could let loose a scream to alert the others, Vine twisted the jerk's neck, then gently lowered him to the floor. He heard a noise behind him and turned to find the younger woman with her hand over Dani Devlin's mouth, telling her to be quiet.

Vine lifted his finger to his mouth, emphasizing quiet. Dani nodded, and the woman with her hand over Dani's mouth backed away. She met his gaze, and a pulse skipped through him. This had to be Admiral Light's friend. She wasn't like anyone else he'd ever met.

"What is going on? How did this happen? We need to go back and help Tom." Dani's eyes flashed with fear, and her cheeks flamed pink. She looked out of control.

"Mrs. Devlin, I suggest you stay with—"

"Leanne," the younger woman said, her voice way too melodic for someone working undercover. She seemed too nice and innocent to be a CIA agent. It wasn't just her red hair or her big blue eyes that attracted him. No, she had something deep inside that made him want to get to know her.

"Stay with Leanne. She'll know how to keep you safe."

Dani shook her head and frowned. "Leanne? She has never been in the military. I would know better."

Vine narrowed his gaze as he stared at Leanne. She looked back at him with the hardened stare of a person who knew what they were doing, while Dani looked half-crazed and out of it. Vine had no clue what Dani knew about this Leanne woman, but this had to be the woman Light had told him about.

"Trust me. Leanne will keep you safe." Vine gave Leanne a short nod. "We'll make sure no one comes in."

"Yes, sir," Leanne said and grabbed Dani's arm, tugging her to the bathroom.

"Where are we going? Shouldn't we be trying to help the senator?" Dani's voice rose as Leanne dragged her to the bathroom.

Vine shook his head. The senator's wife would be no help. She had to know she couldn't do any good, but it seemed like she didn't want to admit she wouldn't be of use for the SEALs. On the other hand, Leanne seemed prepared to do whatever needed to be done for them to succeed.

They moved out, leaving Wig behind to keep up with this area and ensure no one went into the cabin. It may take them all night to get the area secured. They had no idea how many people were out in the woods, and he wasn't sure what the captors' end game was. Killing the senator might be top of their list, but with a CIA agent working undercover, maybe Devlin had something to hide, too.

CHAPTER 3

Jenna listened carefully, trying to pick up any sounds, a scuffle outside, anything that would tell her what was going on. This whole trip felt off. Devlin had met with only one government official in Istanbul, and the meeting wasn't that big of a deal. Then he sprang this trip to the cabins on them without any warning. What was that about? And why had the senator bonded so quickly with the guests who had shown up shortly after they'd arrived? Then they'd been taken captive in the middle of the night. The trip and the senator stank horribly. Everything was wrong.

She needed to know more about the stranger. What country was the man from, and who did he work for? Senator Devlin was dirty, but in the two months she'd been working for his office, she hadn't found anything condemning. She'd known going in this would be a long-term operation. Becoming a senator's aide would take months and maybe years of subterfuge to get the dirt on him she needed to shut him down. To have this happen, something so dramatic at just two months in, was weird.

"We should go check what's going on," Dani said as she stared up at the bathroom ceiling.

Jenna had decided both of them on the floor between the tub and the shower would be the safest place. "No. Stay down. If they start shooting, the tub should protect you."

Dani rolled her eyes. "I don't care. I need to find Tom."

In the two months she'd worked with Devlin, she'd only heard Dani call him Tom one other time. That had been when she'd been angry with him. Was Dani angry with Senator Devlin now? What could he have done to anger her?

Jenna didn't trust Dani, and now she trusted her even less. She needed to find a way to get more inside information from Devlin. She'd found a way to get his email directed to her, and she'd cloned his phone and received all his text messages, but there had to be some other way he was communicating.

She should have found it by now, but the man was tricky.

Even though they'd laid down in the bedroom at the main cabin, they hadn't gotten much sleep. She wasn't surprised when Dani drifted off. They'd been on the floor for about twenty minutes, and it was boring to sit here with nothing to do.

Jenna moved quietly but quickly to the door and slipped out. The man the SEAL had killed earlier was still on the floor in the entryway. Jenna moved to him, searching for a weapon. She found a small handgun tucked into an ankle holster. She also found a knife at his back. The gun he'd been going for had been picked up by the SEALs, emptied of rounds, and taken away.

A part of her thought she should stay here where she wouldn't run into anyone, but another part of her wanted to go out and find the senator. It had been long enough for the SEALs to rescue him, but they'd disappeared as far as she was concerned. Could she trust them, or did she need to take matters into her own hands?

Jenna slipped out the cabin's back door and slid around to the sidewall, searching for movement. She didn't have night vision goggles, but the moon had risen high and was almost full. She could make out the tree line and the other cabins. She made a dash to the closest cabin and stayed in the shadows as she waited for her heart to slow.

A noise behind her almost made her scream, but she held still, listening for more. Two men were speaking in English. At first, she thought they were the SEALs, but one of them had an accent.

"Why did you kill his aide?"

Was that Andrew? Anger made her heat. How could Andrew be working with these people?

"The others know we are serious now. They won't mess with you. Besides, Devlin indicated one of your group was a double-crosser. It had to be him based on how Devlin was acting."

Andrew blew out a breath. "We didn't know if it was him."

"Whatever. So that one woman, do you think we can have a little fun later? The younger one, not his wife."

Blood rushed in Jenna's ears, and she missed the reply. She needed to calm the heck down.

"He's fine with our request, yes?" the man with the accent asked.

"He's happy," Andrew said.

"Good. We'll be in touch later. Our two masters meeting face to face was important."

Jenna missed the reply. She covered her mouth to keep from making a noise. Devlin was helping these people.

"I enjoyed our talk," Andrew said.

"Same. Now, it's time for me to go."

Jenna held her breath as she watched a man she'd never seen walk away to her right as Andrew headed back toward the cabin where Devlin was staying.

Now she knew why they'd come out here. This had been planned. The CIA was missing important communication between Devlin and these terrorists. Birch's death was on Devlin's hands. This operation needed to move forward fast. If she killed the senator, she would have to answer to someone because it wouldn't stay quiet. But who was the senator talking to? She needed to know. The man was despicable, but it seemed like he was above the law.

Jenna was ready to run across to the main cabin when a hand came around her mouth. She tried to jerk away, but she was pulled backward against a hard body.

"It's Vine, one of the SEALs. What are you doing out of the cabin?"

She sucked in air through her nose then blew it out. "It has been almost an hour."

"We had something we had to take care of. Why are you out here?"

"What is going on?"

He turned her so she was facing him. She couldn't make out much, but she caught the moonlight glinting off his eyes. His expression was hard, his lips thinned. She imagined few ever disobeyed his commands and lived to talk about it.

"We have this handled," he said.

"I need—" Jenna caught movement behind him and narrowed her gaze. It was one of the guys who had shot Birch. She moved fast, pulling her gun with her left hand. She fired, hitting him in the neck.

"Shit," Vine cursed.

"Sorry," Jenna said.

"For what? You saved my hide and killed that guy. You have nothing to be sorry about."

Heat washed over Jenna's face. His praise hit her deep and left her feeling like she could hang the moon. Normally, things rolled off her back, leaving her cool as a cucumber, but this man was different.

"We should move his gun," Jenna said.

"True." He held up one finger. "I'm fine. The woman with Devlin shot one of the guys." He nodded then his focus came back to her. "The guys heard that. Thank you again, but you need to get back into that cabin where Mrs. Devlin is."

"I want to go with you and find Devlin. He has a lot to answer for."

"The reality is, he's a US senator."

Jenna blew out a frustrated breath. "Fuck. I need hard evidence."

"You need to go back to that cabin and sit with Dani. She's his wife. Do you honestly think she's not just as dirty as he is? If she is allowed to wander around out here, she could do damage."

Jenna sighed. She would have to trust this man. They had plenty of time to make it to Devlin's cabin, but they hadn't. She didn't think the SEALs were dirty like Devlin, but more than met the eye was going on.

CHAPTER 4

Vine couldn't believe what he'd seen after they'd secured Dani and Leanne in the cabin. Of course, they were using the latest tech in night vision with thermal imaging, allowing him to see the trees through the fog that had rolled in. He and a few members of his team had seen two people leaving the main cabin. Devlin still didn't know his team was on site.

They followed the men's progress, not at all surprised to find two men walking from the trees to meet up with the guys from the cabin.

None of these jerks had a clue the SEALs were watching their every move. He planned on keeping it that way for as long as possible. At least until they figured out what was going on or they were forced to reveal themselves.

His team let everything play out as they stayed out of the way, praying these jerks didn't try to contact the men they'd taken out earlier in the evening. Legs had been able to move close enough to plant a recording device. They wouldn't get everything said, but they would have some form of a recording. Maybe it would be enough to determine what they were planning.

When Vine had seen movement next to the cabin with the women, shock pulsed through him. For a moment, he feared Leanne would enter the cabin where the four men were meeting. She hadn't. Instead, she was beside the cabin when the men stepped out. She'd seemed just as intrigued as he'd been when they'd found the senator's aide chatting comfortably with the other men.

Now it was close to midnight, and the aide was headed back to the main cabin with the man Vine thought was one of the abductors. They'd pulled Wig from the cabin with Leanne and Dani, and now he and Astro were following the two men who'd walked out into the trees.

It was time to break up the party. He'd gone for Leanne, covering her mouth to keep her quiet.

This wasn't some easy rescue. Admiral Light had mentioned he knew Leanne. How well did the admiral know her? Could she be in on whatever Devlin was trying to pull off, or was she innocent? She was undercover, but how covert was she? He had loads of questions and no answers.

She struggled against him, and he pulled her closer. "It's Vine, one of the SEALs. What are you doing out of the cabin?"

Her chest expanded as she gulped in air. "It has been almost an hour."

He almost chuckled at her tone, but he held it in. "We had something we had to take care of. Why are you out here?"

"What is going on?"

"We have this handled."

"I need—"

Suddenly Leanne moved and pulled out her gun. She fired off a shot as he turned to see a man go down.

"Shit."

"Sorry," Jenna said.

"For what? You saved my hide and killed that guy. You have nothing to be sorry about."

He should have been more aware. That guy could

have killed him. This woman distracted the heck out of him.

"We should move that gun," Leanne said.

"True." He held up one finger as Wig spoke to him through the comms.

"Vine, is that you?"

"I'm fine. The woman with Devlin shot one of the guys."

"No way Devlin isn't a terrorist too. Now with all we've found," Wig said.

Vine couldn't really respond to Wig with this woman standing in front of him. "The guys heard that," he explained as she continued to stare at him with a funny look on her face. "Thank you again, but you need to get back into that cabin where Mrs. Devlin is."

"I want to go with you and find Devlin. He has a lot to answer for."

He couldn't believe they were in this situation. How had they fallen into a mission where they were having to consider the senator they were rescuing was dirty? Would he have them killed?

"The reality is he is a US senator."

"Fuck, I need hard evidence," Leanne said.

They all did, but they weren't going to get it right now. "You need to go back to that cabin and sit with

Dani. She's his wife. Do you honestly think she's not just as dirty as he is? If she is allowed to wander around out here, she could do damage."

Leanne let go a heavy sigh. She looked like she was about to leave, but she turned back to him. "Something…" she closed her eyes and shook her head.

"What?" He didn't have time to play games with her. As a SEAL, he knew not everything was what it seemed, and he didn't like getting mixed up in drama. This whole operation had drama written all over it, and he couldn't tell if Leanne was a part of that drama or if she was trying to stop it. "Spill it," Vine commanded.

She met his gaze with a solid look he usually only saw from other military guys. "Something isn't right."

A shiver raced through her, and he wondered what she thought of him and his men. Was her hesitation because she thought they were in on the subterfuge played out by Devlin?

"We figured. That's why we've been taking our time."

Leanne nodded. "There's something deeper going on out here. Something that isn't good for national security. We need to know the identity of the men who walked into the forest."

Vine's lips thinned. "I have two of the best guys in the Navy on it."

"Be careful," Leanne said.

This time a little chuckle escaped his lips. She rolled her eyes. "You know what I mean."

"We're always careful," Vine replied.

She shook her head then looked him up and down. "I don't have your fancy equipment. I'll go back to the cabin."

"You be careful, too." He turned to walk away, but Leanne stopped him again.

"I do believe she's in on it. I'm not one hundred percent, but you need to be prepared for things to turn. And whatever happens, Devlin can't know I contacted Admiral Light."

Vine gave a sharp nod. "We'll find some time to talk later." He took off. When he glanced back, he saw Leanne slipping into the cabin she'd left minutes earlier. His first duty in this fucked up situation was to his men, then he'd make sure he could save Leanne. After that, if the senator did something stupid, it was up to him to survive.

Once they were back on the USS Paul Hamilton, Vine needed to chat with Admiral Light and possibly with Leanne. He wanted to figure out what the heck was going on. If they stayed with the ship all the way to Istanbul, it would take them about twenty hours. In that time, he could find out a lot from this Leanne woman.

"We have an issue," Vine said over the communication device everyone on his team wore.

"No shit," Legs replied. "She was close enough we heard it all. This guy is jerking everyone around."

"I can't wait to hear what's on that recording," Quirk said.

Vine moved closer to the cabin with the senator. They needed a new plan of action.

"The two guys we followed got into a car and took off," Wig said over comms.

"Well, crap," Vine groused. "Come back. We'll figure out our next move."

He met up with everyone but Wig and Astro about twenty yards from the big cabin. They all looked pissed. He could tell from their stances alone they didn't like what was going on.

"Are we right?" Legs asked.

Vine took a sip of water and stared at the sky for a moment. "The senator's aide was meeting with that man who took off in that car. We heard what he said at the end. The senator is in on it. Give me one good reason a senator of the USA would travel to a cabin in the woods in Turkey, be friendly with the guys who captured his wife and aide, and then hold them in another cabin. Why would he stay friendly with a group that apparently killed one of his other aides? We need to hear what is on that device, but we'll need to play it at volume, and I don't want him to know we have any recordings of them."

"We're almost back," Astro said over comms.

"Who knows we're here?" Legs asked.

"Well, the guys we killed. But they ain't talking," Quirk said.

If they hadn't been in the middle of a potentially explosive situation, Vine would have laughed. Quirk didn't disappoint in trying to live up to his name.

"We can't go back to the ship without the senator. His wife knows we're here." Vine turned and stared into the darkness to his left.

"How can we explain our presence?" Legs asked.

"He has a good point," Astro said.

"The senator isn't going to be happy we were called in," Vine said.

"That Leanne woman, she said she didn't want us revealing that she was the one who called this in, but it's going to be revealed at some point," Wig said.

"Specifically, she said she didn't want the senator

knowing she contacted Admiral Light. We don't have to spill that pot of beans," Quirk replied.

Everyone had good points, but they still didn't have a good way to end this situation. Vine wondered if just walking into the cabin with the senator would be enough when gunfire suddenly erupted at the edge of the clearing. The door to the cabin flew open, and one of the hostage-takers stepped out.

"Want me to shoot him?" Wig asked over the comms.

"Shoot to wound," Vine said.

The shot sounded, dropping the guy to the ground. Vine eased his way toward the cabin, fairly certain there was no one else they would have to take down.

"Wig, Astro, report." Vine needed to know what had happened.

Astro came over his comms link. "We found a kid sleeping out in the trees. He popped off two shots at me before he shot himself. I think he's going to bleed out."

"How did he shoot himself?" Vine asked.

"Pistol in his lap," Wig said.

"Shit." This whole thing was getting too messy for Vine. He loved his job, he really did, but this was the type of operation he hated. Someone who was supposed to be dedicated to the USA seemed to be playing a double-cross.

"I shot the dude next to the big cabin in the knee. Approach with caution," Wig said.

Vine and his crew edged closer to the cabin, prepared to take this guy out if he didn't stay down.

"Legs, take care of the guy on the ground. We need answers from him." Vine moved to the cabin, wishing he knew who else was in there. Because he believed the senator to be dirty, he tossed in a flash-bang before moving in.

He followed Minx and Quirk into the cabin, sweeping the room quickly before heading to one of the closed doors. They all knew the score, knew there was something up with the senator. Vine's guys would return fire if shot at. No way were they dying for a dirty senator.

He turned the handle and let the door slide open before sticking out his arm and waving. He half-expected to be shot at. Nothing happened.

Vine used a mirror he had in one of his pockets to look into the room. The senator was stretched out on the bed, hands zip-tied together in front of him. Minx moved in quickly and pulled the senator up, not bothering to remove the zip strips on his hands or the gag tied around his head.

Vine almost rolled his eyes at the senator's antics. His hands were bound in front of him, which he could've done on his own, and the gag tied around his mouth could've easily been done by him. He must believe they were stupid. They'd just seen his aide outside running around the compound, and here Devlin expected them to believe he had been taken captive.

The senator's assistant was in a closet, his hands bound in front of him. Vine had just about had it with these two. He wanted to tell the senator and his aide they knew everything, but they didn't know everything. There was still information they needed to figure out.

Vine helped Devlin outside before roughly cutting off the zip ties binding his wrists.

He didn't help the senator remove the gag in his mouth. The guy Wig shot had been moved where they couldn't see him.

"Oh, thank God. Where is my wife?" Senator Devlin asked.

"She's secure in another cabin. We can head over there now."

Vine needed to get to Leanne and talk to her. He

had a feeling that would have to wait until they were on the USS Paul Hamilton. There was no way they could have a private conversation out here.

After seeing the senator's aide sneaking around, the last thing he wanted was this guy to figure out they knew something was going on. If the senator would go to these lengths to do something dirty, who knew what he would do at home. Senators had powers that could derail programs like the SEAL Teams if they started sticking their noses in where they didn't belong. Vine would have to tread carefully or risk not only his future but the future of the teams.

CHAPTER 5

Jenna had been waiting for the SEALs to enter their cabin. When the door opened, she jumped but settled quickly. Senator Devlin stood behind the first two SEALs, with what looked like concern shining in his eyes. He was doing a great job acting the part of a sad spouse. It took restraint on her part to not fire off questions about the man Andrew had met with in the other cabin. She wanted to know what kind of crap he was playing at. She'd heard the damning evidence, but so far, it was her word against his. He would lie because that's what he was good at.

"Oh, thank God you're okay," Dani said.

Devlin moved to Dani and gave her a hug before pulling back to meet Jenna's gaze. "Thank goodness you're okay, too. I don't know what—" the senator started sobbing, and Jenna wanted to call him on his BS. She knew his tears were fake, just like his morals. The man talked a good game, going on news shows and telling the interviewer how his faith helped him be a good senator. It was all bullshit. If he had faith, it wasn't in God or Jesus.

"We need to clean up and take care of a few things," Vine said.

All but one of the SEALs left, leaving her with the senator and his wife along with Andrew and one of the men from the SEAL team. Jenna couldn't let on that she knew Devlin and Andrew were dirty. She would have to keep that information to herself until she could figure out exactly what they'd been doing.

What were their plans? She should've insisted she stay with Devlin last night, but she sensed they wouldn't have only killed Birch, and she would be dead, too. She wouldn't have texted Admiral Light, and the SEALs wouldn't have shown up here. Who knows what would have happened if she wouldn't have asked Light for help?

"What happens now?" Senator Devlin asked.

The SEAL lifted his chin but didn't say anything for a moment. "I do whatever my commander tells me to do. That's what happens next."

Jenna could tell the guy's answer wasn't going to appease Devlin. She bet Devlin didn't know these men were SEALs. They looked like badasses of the highest order, but Devlin didn't seem to be impressed. The man in the cabin with them was obviously special teams based on his beard and hair length. If Devlin thought this guy was a SEAL, he would be falling all over him, trying to take pictures so he could brag to other members of congress.

In the few months she'd been working for Devlin, she'd figured out he was a pompous jerk. He really thought he should get special treatment above and beyond everyone else. He wasn't serving those he represented in congress. Instead, he expected to be treated like royalty wherever he went.

She liked that the SEALs hadn't jumped all over Devlin and treated him special. Devlin may talk the talk when he was on stage in front of his constituents, but he hated military guys. He'd said more than once when they were in his office, he thought those in the military were stupid. If he thought for a moment he could use this man, Devlin would change his tune and get all buddy-buddy. A regular grunt in the military wasn't useful, but a SEAL would be Devlin's ticket onto the talk show circuit. Devlin ascribed to the idea the more face time he got on TV, the better he was doing.

"I need to contact my people in Washington," Devlin said as he moved to the door.

"No can do," the SEAL said as he held up one hand, blocking Devlin from leaving. "It's too dangerous out there. We wouldn't want you getting shot."

Devlin looked like he was about to say something, then closed his mouth and turned back to his wife. Jenna caught the angry glint in his gaze before he schooled his features and pasted on what he must've thought was a pleasant smile. To Jenna, he looked annoyed, like a bratty teenager who'd been told no.

"It's probably for the best. Who knows how many of those crazy terrorists are out there?"

Jenna had to bite her tongue to keep her from screaming at Devlin. The man knew who was out there. He just didn't know that they'd been neutralized by SEALs. Instead of snapping back at him or bursting out laughing, she headed to the kitchen to fix coffee. There was food in the main cabin, but she doubted they would head over there before leaving.

She needed to grab her phone before they left. She wished she knew Devlin's next move. But she had a part to play if she wanted to stay Devlin's employee. If he got suspicious of her, thinking she was more than just a good assistant, he would can her ass, and then the CIA would have to use other means to get information. Or worse, he'd figure out she was working on getting dirt on him, and he would figure out a way to get her arrested. The last thing she wanted was to spend time in jail.

She remembered when she'd been briefed on the information linking Devlin with the leak that got five hundred soldiers killed. She'd wanted to take him out, not just investigate him. It would be easy. Someone could set up on a tall building and use a fifty-caliber rifle. Anything to get his filthy piece of trash ass off this planet. But there were ways to work around him that didn't involve killing him, and one of those ways was to expose the heck out of him and let his sins be known. If she killed him, he might become a martyr.

Jenna had to calm down. Her anger was too close to the surface. She thought of a calming beach as she poured the first cup of coffee, hiding the anger and pain that made her want to kill Devlin. She turned and faced the group, smiling like nothing was wrong.

"Anyone want coffee?" Jenna asked, modulating her voice to prevent her anger from leaking out.

Devlin and Dani both took a cup of coffee, but the SEAL declined. She didn't want to seem weird in front of Devlin, so she kept her eye contact with the SEAL to a minimum though she really wanted to interrogate him and ask what the heck they were doing to get information on Devlin.

When she'd finished her cup of coffee, the door opened. Vine stepped in, exuding power just by being there. Her heart stuttered a bit. What was that about? Sure, the guy was sexy, but she didn't need sexy in her life.

Because she was in the CIA, she'd taken a very utilitarian approach to relationships. Allowing someone to get close was dangerous and impossible when she played long-term parts like Leanna Armstrong. Then again, it had been years since she'd come face to face with a man who had strength and power like Vine. It wasn't just his muscles either. Vine exuded power.

She watched him, taking in the way he moved, how he observed the room in a quick sweep. When his gaze met Jenna's, a shiver slid through her. Luckily, she was behind Devlin, and he didn't notice her looking at the SEAL.

Vine's gaze held hers for a beat, warming her cold heart. It almost felt like a crust had been broken off the outer layers of her heart. But it hadn't. She couldn't trust anyone here, least of all a very sexy man who made her want to change everything. She couldn't change anything in her life right now. She would stick to the plan. That was the only way she could be sure this monster was gone, and more US citizens weren't killed by the psychopath.

"We're headed out in ten minutes." Vine's gaze swung back to Devlin. "We grabbed your computer, phone, and other electronics from the cabin and packed your bags."

Jenna thought Devlin was going to throw a fit. She saw the anger building behind his eyes. No question Devlin was pissed. Instead of going off on this SEAL, Devlin closed his mouth and gave a curt nod. Maybe Devlin knew he was in a bad spot. It was the first wise thing he'd done in a while.

She watched Vine, keeping aware of every move he made. Had the SEALs searched Devlin's computer for the information she needed? Now she had a reason to get close to him.

Her heart sped up, and she pushed the errant desire away. This wasn't going to turn into a romp. Vine was smart enough to recognize her motivations from a mile away. If she went to him, it had to be the straightforward approach.

First, she needed to get to him on the ship and figure out what he knew. She needed a plan before they were separated. Luckily, she knew Admiral Light. He'd probably be pissed at her for being in the CIA, but he would get over it, maybe.

It only took her a few minutes to shove her stuff into her bag. Dani complained, and Devlin yelled at the SEALs threatening their jobs. His attitude pissed Jenna off. SEALs were known to be an unbending group and didn't bow to anyone. They proved her right once again as they ignored Devlin's threats.

One of the guys came over to her and held out her phone. "This is yours, right?"

Jenna flashed him a smile. "Thank you."

The SEAL winked at her before he turned and stalked off. A sliver of shock wove through her. She met Vine's gaze, and she swore his lips twitched up in a smile.

They weren't walking far, which was good since one SEAL carried Birch on a plank behind them, and the injured abductor was being dragged behind them on a makeshift pallet.

When Dani complained about the conditions on their hike, Devlin snapped at her. The SEALs stayed professional though they told Devlin and his wife to zip their lips, that other people could be out in the forest waiting to kill them.

From experience, Jenna knew the dead would've been lined up, photos taken, the information detailed in an informational report about the military action. Someone in the Navy would file the report with the proper people in Turkey to get this dismissed as a necessary action so the US military wouldn't face any backlash. Knowing what she did now, she wouldn't have called for help. She would've drugged the senator then looked through his bags and computer, praying he didn't remember being drugged. But she would have had to drug everyone else, too. They probably would have ended up dead. She needed to find out who Devlin had met with in secret.

She needed to make fast friends with the SEALs and get the information from them. Based on how territorial they were, this might be one of her most difficult tasks ever.

The ride out to the USS Paul Hamilton seemed a little dicey to Jenna, but the SEALs appeared to have everything under control. Dani had a white-knuckle grip on the rope she'd been told to hold on to, and Senator Devlin looked as pale as a ghost. Jenna had spent her share of time on zodiacs while in the Marines, but that didn't mean she loved this mode of travel. Midway through the boat ride, her stomach pitched enough she thought she would give back the coffee she had consumed almost an hour earlier. It took her a moment of deep breathing to get settled again.

Their captor who'd been shot was still passed out. One of the SEALs kept his eyes on the man, making sure he didn't come to. The SEALs had covered Birch with a tarp that Devlin nor Andrew even looked at. Jenna would miss Birch. Not that they'd been close but seeing him killed had been disturbing.

Being in the military and then the CIA, she'd seen some messed up stuff, but Devlin took the cake. The things he did, the way he did them, made her skin crawl. That he could wake up in the morning and look at himself in the mirror after knowingly having five hundred US military personnel killed amazed her.

She'd once almost made a mistake in a hot zone, and the guilt had eaten at her for days. Even now, just thinking how something she could have done might have gotten one of her military buddies killed made her squeamish. Sure, she killed for the CIA, but most of her responsibilities were information gathering, not killing. And the people she'd taken out had been like Devlin, reckless jerks who didn't care about others. There were things in her life she wished had turned out differently, but she knew she'd tried hard to keep Americans alive, and everything she'd done was in service of her country and not herself.

When they approached the destroyer class ship, relief filled her. In her original text to Admiral Light, she explained that she was using the name Leanne, and she hoped he didn't give away her true identity. As far as the US government was concerned, Leanne Armstrong was real. They'd given her a history, planted little crumbs about her identity back to grade school.

She wanted to kiss the deck when she stepped onto the naval ship, but she didn't. A seaman led her, Andrew, Dani, and Devlin to a set of quarters where they were told they could wash up and sleep. After she showered then dressed in fresh clothes, Jenna opened the door to her cabin and wasn't surprised to find a young man stationed in the hall, blocking their access to the rest of the ship. The Navy would never allow a civilian to walk around a ship involved in an operation. Even Senator Devlin wouldn't be given free access. He and Dani would have to follow a guide if they allowed them out of their room at all.

"If there's any way possible, I'd like to talk to master chief Vine." Jenna flashed the guy a smile and hoped she would be given an audience.

The young man who probably had never spoken to Master Chief Vine, much less any other SEAL, nodded and flashed a shy smile at her. "Yes, ma'am. I'll see what I can do." This guy must've worked in customer service or grew up in the south. He was charming, and his smile disarming. She bet that was why this guy was chosen to be placed down here. Admiral Light knew he had to do a little butt-kissing for the senator, but this guy could tell you no and make you think it was your idea.

Jenna doubted Vine would hear about her request, but the way this young man in front of her smiled was meant to make her feel like her request was a top priority. She didn't blame the guy. As far as he knew, she was a lowly aide to a senator. Certainly not anyone worth paying attention to. She wasn't going to start handing out demands because she had a plan forming in her head that hopefully would get her the information she needed.

She obviously wouldn't be allowed to run around

the ship, so Jenna stretched out and dozed off. She was surprised when someone knocked on her door.

Jenna rolled out of bed, careful not to bang her head on the bunk above her, and went to the door, pulling it open. The young seaman she'd seen earlier had been replaced with an older guy who didn't seem to have the same level of customer service.

"You're wanted on the bridge. Go with him."

She looked behind the guy and noticed a short dude with wide shoulders. She followed the man who was maybe an inch shorter than her. She had to speed up as he ran up the stairs like a pro. The rough sea made her almost miss a few steps, and she had to take it slower. The guy did slow when he realized she wasn't used to running up and down the stairs on a ship in rough seas. She swore he sneered, but she didn't hold it against him. His whole day had probably been thrown off by having to fetch her. She'd hated tasks like that when she'd been in the Marines. Having to handle people wasn't her idea of fun.

The door to the bridge was opened for her, and she stepped in, resisting the urge to salute. She wasn't in the military, and she had to play the part the CIA had given her. Leanne Armstrong had never been in the military.

Admiral Light lifted his eyebrows and frowned at her, then jerked his head toward the door to her right. Jenna moved to follow and was surprised to see Vine along with another one of the SEAL members already in the room. This might be easier than she'd first thought it would be.

CHAPTER 6

Vine closed the door behind the woman and stood so he would block anyone from entering. He expected Light to start off with pleasantries. Instead, Admiral Light turned to Leanne, his scowl deep as he pointed his finger at her.

"What in God's name is going on? You ask for help, tell me to call you a different name, and you bring my SEALs into this mess that's got trouble written all over it. I've got a master chief telling me he thinks a senator might have committed treason. Treason? What in the hell did you get yourself into, young lady?"

The woman's lips spread into a huge smile before she reached out and squeezed Admiral Light's arm. "It's good to see you, too. If I'd known what Devlin was doing, I would've had backup arranged. The trip to the cabin was unexpected. It wasn't on his itinerary. And I'm on his team because normal channels were ineffective."

Admiral Light narrowed his eyes and shook his head. "Normal channels?"

"He was under investigation that ended last year. The DOJ decided against seeking further information on what Devlin had done. He knew about the DOJ's interest and must have pulled strings. He doesn't know about my involvement."

Vine took in the way Light shook his head in disgust. He wasn't happy with her, like a father disappointed in a child. There was something between them. Some affection displayed like they were related, and she seemed to view him as a kind uncle or something like that. He knew this woman wasn't Light's child, and she was too old to be his grandchild.

"I knew you leaving the military would lead to something like this. The CIA? That place is dangerous. Your father wouldn't like this at all."

Vine wondered who her father was. First, he needed to figure out her real name. Then he would investigate her. There had to be a reason behind her being good friends with Admiral Light.

The woman's lips thinned, and she rolled her eyes. Vine had never seen anyone act this way toward an admiral. It was oddly entertaining to see this woman go up against Admiral Light. She wasn't afraid of him at all.

She huffed out a breath and crossed her arms over her chest. "Well, he's dead. I'm doing what I think is right. I serve my country. I make sure terrorism can't take hold when I'm involved. I may not be perfect, and yes, I'm in danger, but somebody has to do this. We knew Devlin was up to something, but we weren't sure what."

"Well, we don't have time to figure it out right now." Admiral Light glanced at his watch, then shook his head. "In fact, you three need to get out of here. Vine, take her down the way you two came up. Get her back to her room without Devlin or his wife seeing you all. Now I have to treat a sorry-ass senator like he's cream of the crop. Shit, I hate politicians."

"Daniel, be careful. Devlin is dirty." she said as she moved close and gave the admiral a quick hug.

Vine hadn't ever heard anyone call Admiral Light by his first name. No one on the ship would have dared say it if they even knew his name. Light hugged her back, closing his eyes and sighing before he kissed the top of her head like a father would. Yeah, Vine needed to know who she was and what her deal was.

"You, too, sweetheart," Light said. "And check-in. I don't want to hear that you were killed by a jerk like Devlin. I need to know where you are now that I know you're in the CIA."

She nodded, then turned. Vine thought he might have seen a bit of a tear in her eyes. That didn't last long because once they were out the door, the hard glint came back. She was intense, more like one of his SEAL buddies than any of the women he'd known in the Navy.

"Follow us, and we'll get you back to your quarters."

The three of them took off, moving quickly from the bridge to the stairwell he and Astro had taken earlier. They had gone down two flights of stairs when Leanne put her hand on his arm and stopped him.

He looked into her wide blue eyes, and for a moment, he was transfixed by how innocent she looked. His heart surged, and a wave of protectiveness washed over him. But he knew any woman in the CIA wasn't innocent. She had seen things just like he and his team had.

"You have information," she said. "We need to figure out what is going on."

A crew member came running down the stairs and raced around them, running down the next set of steps. They were out in the open, and this wasn't any place to talk. Her quarters were right next to Senator Devlin's, so they couldn't take the chance of speaking there. No way would he invite her to their quarters, mainly because he knew that would get them in trouble faster than anything else. This woman had Admiral Light's protection, which Vine didn't want to overstep. Sure, he was a SEAL, but pissing off an admiral would be stupid.

And if it got back to Light that he had taken her into his private quarters here on the ship, there was no telling what the man would do. Not that Vine would do anything with her, but just the implication would be enough to get him in the hot seat.

"We can't talk here. And we don't know each other. You don't know if you can trust me, and I don't know if I can trust you," Vine said.

The woman glanced around and gave a sharp nod when another seaman ran down the stairs and dashed around them.

"Where are you stationed?" She drew him in with her intensity. He would be lying if he said he didn't want to get to know her better. She would challenge him, which was good. He needed a good challenge to keep him on his toes. He didn't want someone who would do whatever he wanted. He wanted a woman who would keep him sharp.

Vine realized he was getting too into her. He pushed the interest away, knowing it would only get him in trouble. "Hawaii."

She flashed him a bright smile. "Perfect. I'll take a leave of absence after we return home. We have to figure this out. I think this is bigger than him trading state secrets for money."

Vine gave a sharp nod and turned, wondering what he was getting himself into. He should turn everything over to her and walk away, but he didn't want to walk away. There was something about her that intrigued him. Now he just had to figure out how much trouble this would cause if it turned out to be bigger than either one of them could handle.

CHAPTER 7

Jenna stepped off the plane in Oahu. She drew in a deep breath and closed her eyes, wondering what in the hell she was doing living in DC. She had money and had invested wisely. She'd rented cheap places instead of living high on the hog and saved her money. DC had nothing on Hawaii, and she could see why people stayed in this beautiful paradise.

She had a job to do, and though Senator Devlin thought she was in Hawaii to chill out and get her head on straight after the terrible terrorist attack they'd gone through, she was here to get to the bottom of what had happened in Turkey.

Before leaving the states, she'd found Vine's phone number and address. She knew his real name was Jason Chase and that he lived near Makakilo.

Before she called him and let him know she was there, she planned on staking out his neighborhood.

Hunger gnawed, so she stopped at a restaurant in a shopping mall on the way over. After getting food and taking a few minutes to freshen up in the restroom, she felt better. To cover her tracks, she'd reserved a room at the Marriott on the beach in the Ko Olina area. If Devlin checked into where she was staying, he would find her reservation, and hopefully, that would be enough for him to believe she really was there on vacation.

Jenna knew Jason drove a three-year-old gray pickup truck with dark windows and a trailer hitch. When she drove past his place, she didn't see his truck. She found a spot where she could see him drive into the neighborhood and sat back to relax. She didn't know how long she would be but figured it would be a few hours before he came home.

She'd slept on the plane, knowing she would need to be awake while watching for him to come home. It was boring sitting in this neighborhood waiting for him to drive up. Sleep threatened but she counted birds at first then started thinking about where she would retire as she watched for Vine. She was glad no one had called the police on her or asked her what she was doing here. It would be awkward to explain.

After a few hours, she heard the rumble of his truck before she saw it. She wasn't surprised when he stopped in front of her car, then hopped out and strode over. The man was smart, and he had made her within seconds.

He moved to the driver's side and placed his forearms on the roof of her car, waiting a beat before he leaned in. He didn't smile or make any pleasantries. Instead, he narrowed his eyes and waited for her to speak.

Jenna tried to push away her lust, but the man looked too good. He had just showered based on the fresh soap scent that blew into her car in the wind. She swallowed over her desire and pushed it away, trying to appear unaffected by him. She figured she had lost that battle, and there was no question he knew she was fascinated.

"Have you looked at the information you got off Devlin's computer?"

Jason stood and glanced around before speaking. "Your eyes are brown."

"This is real. Before, I was wearing colored contacts."

He lifted his eyebrows. "The hair?"

"I'm really blonde, or maybe I'm gray by now, but I was blonde before I went into the CIA and started changing my appearance."

He lifted his chin and turned back to his truck before he glanced back. "I guess you know which house is mine. We'll talk there."

Jenna pulled on her seatbelt and started the car, deciding he was right. It would be best to talk at his place. She parked in his driveway beside his truck and stepped out of the car to follow him inside. She waited on his porch as he grabbed his gear out of his truck.

He approached her, his sunglasses hiding his eyes so she didn't know exactly where he was looking though she felt the weight of his stare. He moved to his door and set his bags down, then turned to face her.

"Before you step into my house, I want to know your real name and the truth about anything else that is fake about you."

As an operative, she didn't normally give out that information. But he was in danger all the time, and she knew his information. It was only fair he knew her name.

"Jenna Mettler. My father, Admiral Shawn Mettler, was in charge of the ship Admiral Light served on thirty years ago when he first joined the Navy. My father met him during one of their tours and took a liking to Daniel. I was a child and knew Daniel because he came over to our house for picnics and football games when they weren't deployed. It may have seemed like an odd relationship, my father being a commander and then an admiral and Light being in ensign then a lieutenant, but my father thought Light would make a good admiral one day. I don't know how he saw it back then, but he saw something in Light that he liked. So now you know that about me and how I know Admiral Light."

Jason scratched his chin and looked her up and down. "Your hair and eye color, anything else fake?"

"Nope, right now, what you see is what you get. I served for three years in the Marines before I was approached to be an agent. I've trained, but I'm not the assassin kind of CIA agent. I'm more the woman everyone ignores and talks business in front of. I collect secrets and get information to the military so they can go in and do missions."

Jason stared at her, then shrugged before turning to open the door. He let her in and headed to his kitchen to grab a glass.

"Would you like any water?" Jason called out as

she looked around his house, taking in the mostly bare walls.

"Thank you, yes. It was a long flight, and I'm dehydrated."

"What did you expect us to find on Devlin's computer?"

Jenna stepped into the kitchen and noticed the large table with six chairs. Did someone else live with him? She took the glass of water from Jason and kept her eyes on him as she drank. Before coming out here, she'd done her research and knew Jason was all about doing what was right. Not once in his military career had he crossed the line into doing something questionable. He was a SEAL, but he'd never blurred the lines like a few SEALs had recently.

"You didn't answer my question. So, does working for the CIA mean you trust no one?" Jason asked.

"Three years ago, four bombs went off on a military base in Europe. Five hundred men and women on that base died. That explosion set off a flurry of investigations. During one of those investigations, we found information. An insider helped the terrorist get inside. They helped set up the conditions for those bombs to go off and kill so many people. It took over a year of work to find out who had leaked the information. When I found the data tying Senator Devlin to the terrorist who set those bombs, I didn't believe it at first. It was hard to come to grips with the reality of one of our senators betraying the United States."

Jason set his glass down and curled his hands into fists. It took him a few seconds to look up and meet her gaze. The anger in his eyes scorched her soul.

"How sure are you on that intelligence?"

Jenna set her glass down and met Jason's solid stare. "I personally went back through the information and checked those connections. Devlin is very dirty. Killing the five hundred military personnel isn't the only thing he's done. He has enough sway to stop investigations in the Department of Justice. That's why I am looking into him. The FBI can't touch him. We need solid evidence if we want to take him down. But first, we really need to stop him from killing more of our own people."

Jason blew out a breath and moved to the den, dragging his hand through his hair before he turned to stare at her. "If what you are saying is true, then we may not be able to stop him."

Jenna took a step closer to Jason, worry exploding through her. "Why? What did you find?"

"We found something tying him to a group of mercenaries operating out of Qatar. But we don't know what they are planning. He's slippery and dangerous."

Jenna blew out a breath and closed her eyes, shaking her head. This was going to get ugly. She didn't know if they could stop the snowball rolling down the hill, but they would have to try, or everything they knew would be a thing of the past.

CHAPTER 8

Vine still didn't know whether to trust this woman or blow her off. Now he had her name and could investigate her. They were constantly looking for ways to break open terrorist networks. Most of his life as a SEAL consisted of either rescuing people from terrorists or cracking open their operations. Then this had fallen into their lap.

He couldn't believe their luck. They had to tread carefully since Devlin was tied to the evidence. Again, he glanced at Jenna, wondering if he could trust her. There was something between them, but sexual attraction meant nothing more than his dick wanted to play. Deep inside, he knew whatever was brewing between them wasn't just sex. The few times he looked into her eyes, whether they were blue or brown, he'd felt a connection pulling at his soul. He shouldn't focus on his desire. They had a job to do. The group in Qatar might not do anything, or they might launch an operation next week.

Still, he felt uncomfortable with her in his space, like an itch he couldn't scratch. Few women were allowed in his home. Since moving to Hawaii, he'd not allowed any woman here. Instead, he'd gone to their place. But this woman got under his skin. She was attractive in a way that made him want to do whatever she wanted. He'd dated better looking women in the past, but they'd done nothing for him. No, this thing between them was deeper than the surface. He liked the way her eyes shined when she spoke about taking down Devlin, and the energy coming off her. She would be a challenge. One he couldn't afford right now. Besides, she lived in DC, and he was here, in this beautiful paradise he loved.

"Why are you here?" Vine asked, hoping his interest in her stayed hidden.

She blew out a breath. "I don't like injustice. I've been watching this mess for a while. Devlin is a piece of shit. I hate him. I don't want him to win."

Vine kept his distance, studying her every move. "The department of justice didn't think he was worth their time."

"That bast—" Jenna cleared her throat and shook her head. "Excuse me. Devlin is buddy-buddy with the second in line at the justice department. He can influence what they take on and who they investigate."

Vine moved into the den and stood with his arms crossed over his chest as he studied her. She watched him, too. Her body coiled tight with energy. Would she turn on him? That was the big question. He'd met a few CIA guys and decided they needed Jesus or something in their lives. They were always searching, playing their informants, trying to get ahead as they crushed others beneath them. Vine knew without a doubt one of the CIA dudes would have sold Vine and his team out if it meant he got recognition. But Jenna seemed different, more open, less of a stabbing in the back type of person.

She moved fast and was only inches from him. He'd been distracted by her beauty, thinking of how soft her cheek looked. She stared up at him with wide brown eyes filled with trust. He had little doubt he could crush her. She might have some moves, but he bet she got out of tricky situations with weapons and hired muscle. Based on her stance, she looked like she knew he could take her out with a few moves, and yet, here she was in his house without a weapon on her, standing so close he could easily end her life.

"You do know I hear curse words all day long."

Her lips twitched up a little on the side. "You are in the Navy."

Her voice had gone low, seductive. He wasn't sure she'd meant to be so alluring because she moved back an inch.

"Why did you come to me?"

Her nostrils flared, and her cheeks turned a little pink. Her gaze flicked down to his chest. What was that about? Did she have the hots for him?

"You have the information I need." Jenna's gaze was back on his, and he had seen desire flickering in her depths.

"You could have gone to my superior. You could have met me on base." Having her here, alone, was tempting. He shouldn't push it. She was alluring, but he needed to concentrate on why she'd showed up.

The slight nod was almost imperceptible. "True. But I don't trust Devlin. If I'd showed up on base and Devlin found out about it, I'd be toast, and so would you. He's suspicious. I guess that's because he's playing everyone."

Vine crossed his arms over his chest, so he didn't reach out and touch her. "So, what do we do now?"

"Have you listened to the recording?"

Vine and his team had been delayed in returning to base. It happened from time to time, but this time he'd been disappointed. They'd just gotten back yesterday evening, and then they'd checked in today to give their report. They weren't due back at base for another four days. They had time to look into the recording now, and he guessed that's what he would spend the next few days doing.

"Not yet."

Her eyebrows shot up, and her mouth fell open for a second. "Why not?"

"We had an issue."

"I need to see what you have and hear that recording."

"Listen, maybe this is a job for the big boys."

Now he'd done it. Anger flashed in her eyes, and the hidden tiger came out. He swore she growled before she placed both hands on her hips and tried to stand taller. His stomach tightened as he watched the anger roll over her. God, that was sexy. He wanted to push more of her buttons and get another reaction just to see how marvelous she looked.

"The big boys? Who do you think I am? I'm not some wide-eyed ingénue who's never been around the block. I've done my time in the trenches both in battle and in DC. This could save lives, and you're going to give me the information one way or another."

Vine burst out laughing. "There's the CIA agent I was expecting. Ready to stab me in the back to get what you want."

She didn't back down. Instead, she moved closer, butting her chest up against him like she planned on fighting him. She was gutsy and sexy in a way that made his dick hard.

Few men would physically challenge him. The fire in her eyes made him want to see how far he could push her. He wanted to feel fire from her, let it consume them until they were hot and sweaty, rolling around with nothing but their sweat separating them.

"I'm doing this to save lives. How dare you think I would stab you in the back? If anything, you're the one—"

Vine moved fast, spinning her so her back was up against the wall. He held her carefully, trying not to injure her. For a second, he thought he'd pushed too far. But then the shock on her face was replaced with a wicked smile that made him think she liked it.

He lowered his head and moved in close so his

lips were at her ear. "We could go head-to-head. Biggest badass wins."

Silence stretched between them, and he was about to pull back when Jenna licked up the column of his neck and nipped at his earlobe. A shiver raced through him, and he let up just enough for her to shove him away.

"You aren't playing fair," Jenna said.

"Neither are you. Now then, how about we both lay all our cards on the table?"

Jenna's lips turned down in a frown. "I laid mine out already."

"You're holding back." Vine crossed his arms over his chest to keep from grabbing her. Fireworks had gone off when he'd touched her, and his cock wanted some action. Shit, that lick from her tongue had almost done him in. He suppressed a shiver, trying not to let on he would get on his knees and make all her wet dreams come true.

"I'm not holding anything back," Jenna said.

Vine lifted his eyebrows then rolled his eyes. "I can tell when you're lying."

Jenna's lips thinned, and her eyes narrowed. She also had her arms crossed over her chest, and he wondered if she wanted to reach out and grab him like he wanted to grab her. Maybe he was just sadistic. He shouldn't want her like this. He didn't even know her.

When he had first joined the Navy, he'd been the type of guy to hop into bed and roll around with any woman who came his way. Then he matured and realized how toxic bed-hopping was to his own psyche. It wasn't that he didn't like sex. He enjoyed sex as well as the next man, but he didn't enjoy having his heart ripped out or his life turned upside down because the woman he'd gone to bed with jerked him around like a feral dog on a leash.

When he had first become a SEAL, he'd witnessed one of the guys who was a legend taken down by a woman he dated. The guy was great in battle and on missions but the women he dated made his life hell. The guy had lost it and ended up having to drop out of the Navy after he'd done something that should have ended up with him in jail. It sucked for the guy, but Vine had learned an important lesson. He stopped picking up random women at bars. He was careful who he slept with, careful who he took home. He made sure the women understood he was a one-night stand, no phone numbers exchanged or expectations offered.

"What are you hiding from me?" Vine demanded,

trying to take his mind off the way she'd felt pressed up against him.

Jenna narrowed her gaze even more, and her lips turned down into a frown. They stared at each other for a long moment. He had to keep his defenses up so he didn't reach out and caress her shoulder. Then he saw her resolve crumble.

"You know we're trying to withdraw from Afghanistan and Iraq. We've seen movement in a few of the cells we are watching. One of our guys on the ground in Iraq was found dead. It was only three weeks ago, so the intelligence we have on it isn't solid yet. We haven't released any of this information to the military yet. We're trying to prevent something like what happened before."

Vine didn't know if he should scream at Jenna or throw up. He remembered when he heard about the bombs that killed five hundred US soldiers. He had been in San Diego at a friend's house. They'd been drinking and staying up late playing video games when the news came in. No one had known. There'd been no intelligence briefings hinting at a terrorist attack on base.

"For the last time, did you know about it? Did the CIA know a base was going to be attacked?"

The anger disappeared from Jenna's face. She

stepped closer, placing her hand on his shoulder. He wanted to roll off her touch as anger and lust combined, making it hard to think. He could pitch a fit and shatter whatever connection had woven between them. He didn't. Instead, he stared into her eyes, watching the sadness grow.

"I didn't know, and the people over me didn't know. I'm fairly certain no one knew it would be that bad. I can't say that not one agent had any idea a terrorist attack would happen on a base, but no one knew it would be so devastating."

He wiped his hand over his face, then dropped his head back and stared up at the ceiling. Her gentle touch affected him. He wanted more. "You want me to trust you, and then you tell me someone at the CIA knew about that attack."

"I'm not a mind reader. Everything I dug into, everything I found said that no one knew. But I know actions can be hidden. Do I trust everyone at the CIA? No. Do I think it's our best bet to stop terrorists? Hell yes. I will do everything I can to make sure no one dies from terrorist action when we start to pull out from those bases."

Vine wanted to believe her. He wanted to think they could stop extreme atrocities from happening. He knew that wasn't always possible. Based on what she said, there was a potential hit planned against the US military. He owed it to his brothers and sisters in arms to try to stop this.

Working with Jenna would be hard. She was CIA, and for some stupid reason, he was attracted to her like a moth to a flame. The last thing he needed or wanted was a girlfriend who was a spy. But his body didn't care what she did for a job. His fingers itched to hold her, and his lips longed to trail kisses across her soft skin, finding secret places that made her cry out his name.

He could do this. He could work with her and not lose himself, or he hoped he could. Because losing himself in her seemed like a fine thing to do.

CHAPTER 9

Jenna knew she was playing a dangerous game. Jason intrigued her, and she didn't have time to investigate the desire he was throwing off. Before, when they'd been in Turkey and then on the ship, she'd been distracted but still had felt something like lust drawing her to him. Then he'd taken off before she'd left the ship. She'd wondered if she would ever see him again. Sure, she had his information, but he was a SEAL, and he knew how to hide from her if he wanted.

She looked around his place, noting there was only one photo of him with other guys. It must have been when he'd finished BUDs or something else that called for a celebration. They all had bottles of beer in their hands, and they were smiling, except one guy. She wondered who he was, not enough to ask at the moment, but eventually, she'd find out.

His call to his friends must have connected because he was talking low, telling them to come over with the stuff. She hoped that stuff was the documents they'd found on Devlin's computer.

She should take everything they had and leave. Honestly, if anyone other than a SEAL team had the information, she would have broken in and taken it. She respected the SEALs and what they could do too much to invade their space. Also, she could use their help. Devlin was a tough nut to crack. He wouldn't go down easily, and she needed to cut him off at the ankles. If she didn't, he would just rear his ugly head again and again until someone cut him down.

"I need to eat. Have you had dinner?" Vine asked.

Jenna shook her head. "I'm not hungry, thank you, though. It was kind of you to ask."

"You'll need to sleep. Where is your hotel?"

"Not far from here on the beach. If Devlin looks into where I'm staying, he'll believe I'm on vacation. It's the Marriott in Ko Olina."

Vine nodded, then left the room. The door closed down the hall. She guessed he was changing clothes and trusted her enough to leave her alone in his house. She grabbed another glass of water and drank it before finding the bathroom.

When she was washing her hands, she looked at herself in the mirror and thought she looked terrible. No wonder Devlin had agreed she should take a break. Dark circles ringed her eyes, and her skin looked pasty, like she had aged five years in the last few weeks. Lack of sleep and increased worry had drained her. This post as Devlin's assistant would be her last. She needed a break. She didn't want Devlin or men like him to win, so she had stayed with the CIA though she was ready to take life easier.

She stepped out of the bathroom and almost ran into Vine. He'd changed into shorts and a T-shirt that clung to his chest. Without even thinking about what she was doing, her tongue snaked out and she licked her lips. A smile flitted over Vine's mouth, making heat spread through her. She didn't like that this man could read her so easily. Then again, this man brought out reactions she normally could control. Just being in his presence made her react.

"The guys will be here in just a few minutes. I'm going to eat some food. Are you sure you don't want any?"

"Thanks, but I'm good." Jenna moved to the den and took a seat on the couch, closing her eyes for just a moment. She woke to the sound of men talking. Slowly she opened her eyes, unsure where she was. Then it all came back. She'd flown to Hawaii and was in Jason's house waiting on his friends to arrive.

She'd slept on the plane, but she'd been in first class and had booked the ticket as Leanne Armstrong. No one knew who she was. Usually, she didn't relax around other people. These SEALs had the ability and the knowledge to take her down and dispose of her. But with Jason, it was different. She trusted him for some strange reason.

She stood and stretched. Jason stepped into the room along with two other men. Their gazes narrowed, and they crossed their arms over their chests. She imagined they'd dealt with the CIA before and didn't trust easily.

"This is Wig and Astro." Vine didn't tell her who was who. She guessed she would have to sort it out on her own.

Jenna stepped closer to them and reached out to shake their hands. "My name is Jenna, and thank you for doing this."

The tallest of the two took her hand and flashed a smile. "I'm Robert, but the guys call me Wig." Robert had blonde hair and blue eyes, and a dimple when he smiled. She bet he had to beat women off with a stick with his all-American boy-next-door looks. She imagined he could charm the pants off any woman he wanted.

"It's nice to meet you. Thank you for saving us in Turkey."

Robert shrugged like what they had done was no big deal. "It's our job. Were supposed to do that."

The other guy stuck out his hand for her to shake. "I'm Forest. The guys call me Astro."

Jenna shook his hand, wondering why his parents and named him Forest. She was sure he probably had taken a lot of unnecessary abuse just based on his name.

Robert chuckled. "We were going to call him Gump when we met him, but Forest is probably the smartest guy in the Navy. Though he can't play baseball worth a damn. It's how he got his name."

Jenna lifted her eyebrows as she stared at Robert. "I don't get it. Why Astro if he can't play baseball?"

"Because he's from Houston. You know the Houston Astros. He failed so badly at playing the game when he first joined the Navy that Astro stuck with him. Also, he's really smart and knows astrophysics. He has his pilot's license. If we need him to, he can fly a helicopter to get us out of a tough spot."

"That is impressive. I guess it's lucky they have you on their team," Jenna said.

Forest's cheeks turned a little pink, and he shook his head. "No, I'm the lucky one. They're the greatest group of guys I've ever known."

Jenna had looked up these guys before she had flown to Hawaii, so she knew Forest was an officer and had graduated from the Naval Academy with top marks. The guy was wicked smart, and he would probably have his own team soon. His only drawback was he was young. But that would change, and soon, he would be moving up the ranks and leading.

"We should get started," Robert said.

"Have you all looked at any of it?" Jenna asked.

Forest shrugged. "I read over some of the files we'd transferred from his computer to this thumb drive. There wasn't much there, but I only skimmed. I'm sure we'll find more the deeper we look."

They set up in the den, Jenna taking a seat on the couch. She went into work mode and ignored everything around her. They searched, reading over their section of files for hours. When she'd exhausted her portion, she sat back and stared up at the ceiling. It seemed like they'd gone through everything, but Jenna felt like they had missed something. They needed more but weren't finding it.

"There has to be something," Jason growled in frustration.

"Let's listen to the audio again. Maybe we missed something." Jenna closed her eyes as Robert hit play on the recording. Unfortunately, they hadn't placed the audio in a good spot because none of them knew what they had been walking into when they arrived in Turkey. If she had known Devlin had planned to meet a contact at those cabins, she would've sent a team ahead to wire the place for audio and video.

Robert hit pause and sat back, shaking his head. Jenna hopped up and paced around the room.

"It's my fault." She bit into her thumbnail, taking her aggression out on the poor thing. "I should've known more was going on. I didn't expect the side trip to a set of cabins in Turkey. I should have figured it out, but I didn't."

"It's not your fault." Vine stood and turned to face her.

"Well, whose is it?" Jenna yelled. She blew out a breath and raised one hand in a plea for forgiveness. "I'm sorry. I'm just frustrated."

"It's Devlin's fault," Vine said as he stepped closer. "He is the only one responsible for his actions. He lied about his intentions. I know you had a job to do, but you weren't given enough time or the information you needed."

Jenna plopped down on one of the kitchen chairs Forest had pulled into the den and buried her head in her hands as frustration ground through her. She sat up but didn't meet their gaze. "The worst part is I think he thought Birch was the plant. He knew he was being watched, and he killed Birch because of me. He didn't know I was the one working for the CIA."

"This is messed up," Robert said as he stood and headed into the kitchen.

"This is why don't like politicians," Jason said.

"I understand they are necessary, but I don't like them either." Forrest sat back and let out a heavy sigh.

"What are we going to do?" Jason asked.

The guys shrugged and met Jenna's gaze. She couldn't hold them to any promises they had made. They were military, not CIA. Sure they were trained to defend the country, but they weren't prepared to take on assholes like Devlin in settings like DC.

"I can't hold you all to anything you promised. This is going to get messy."

"We do messy well," Robert said.

Jenna was about to tell him no, that he didn't

need to help, when Jason moved to stand in front of her. He crossed his arms over his chest, and a deep frown pulled his lips down.

"You aren't getting rid of us that easily. We said we would help you, and we will. Now then, let's look deeper, go further. Forrest, use that big brain of yours and figure out if there is something hidden in the files we downloaded. Jenna, use your connections to find us the information we need. If this jerk can be stopped, we're going to do it."

Jenna drew in a slow breath. Hope was restored. Maybe they would fail, but she had an idea that they just might succeed.

CHAPTER 10

Vine had a feeling they were at the end of the line. They needed more information, but to get that information, they would need to travel to DC. He didn't want Jenna to leave so soon, but if they couldn't get something from the files they'd taken from Devlin's computer, they would be totally out of luck.

Jenna looked like a mess. It wasn't really late their time, but she'd flown in from DC after flying back from Turkey. He shouldn't get involved with her. It wasn't right. She was in DC, and he was out here. He'd never leave the Navy—at least not any time soon. He had years before he would retire. He loved being a SEAL, and when he wasn't strong enough or young enough to be a SEAL, he'd move to Coronado and become an instructor or something like that. Maybe he'd become a Bull Frog, staying in the Navy longer than anyone else he knew. A woman had no place in his life.

"You should get some sleep," Robert told Jenna.

She stood and glanced around. "I'm sorry I dragged you all into this."

"No, we're glad to help. We'll see what we can figure out. Maybe some sleep will give you a different perspective," Forest said.

Vine wanted to hug her, but they weren't close friends, and she wasn't his girlfriend. He had no right to touch her.

"Call when you wake up," Jason said.

"Sure." Jenna nodded.

She seemed like she wanted more, but what could they have? A few nights of mindless sex and then nothing. DC was so far east their time zones wouldn't make sense. She'd be getting up for work, and he'd be dead asleep. After his workday ended, she'd be sleeping. They wouldn't talk or anything. It would suck. No, it would be better to ignore the pull and stay sane. If he touched her, he'd fall for her. Already the connection he felt was amazing.

"Text us when you get to your hotel," Forest said.

Vine should have thought of that. Maybe he

should follow her and make sure she got to the hotel okay. He was about to bring it up when she laughed.

"You guys know I'm in the CIA. I've traveled around the world alone. I know what trouble looks like."

"Sure," Forest said. "That doesn't mean we don't take the safety of our friends seriously."

"I'll drive behind you," Vine spit out so fast everyone turned to stare at him.

"No." Jenna shook her head. "That's ridiculous."

Now he was on a mission to take care of her. "No, it's not, and you know it. Just accept our help. I'll follow you to the hotel and make sure you get there safe. You're tired, it's late. Tomorrow we'll let you come over here on your own."

"Don't you have to be on base or something?" Jenna asked.

"No, we're off for four days," Robert said.

"Four?" Jenna sounded incredulous as she looked from Forest to Robert.

Forest nodded. "Yeah, we've been going hard. They make us take a break every once in a while. Otherwise, we burn out. Come over in the morning, and we'll get breakfast as we talk over our options."

Jenna grabbed her things and glanced around. "I feel like I forgot something."

"You didn't bring much in," Vine said.

Her teeth sank into her lower lip as she glanced around. "No. I think I'm just off because of travel, and I feel safe with you all. Usually, I don't let my guard down, but I'm not usually in the presence of men with honor."

Vine's cheeks heated as his chest expanded. He had it bad for her. He needed to get it through his thick skull that she would never be his. Their lives were too different. He knew better than to go after something he would never have.

"Let's go," Vine said. He needed a few moments to recover from her words. At least he wasn't wearing tight shorts, so his friends didn't see the half-chub threatening to go full hard. His team would rib him, no question about that. They had to have noticed his reaction to Jenna, how his cheeks had heated. No telling what they would say to him once he returned.

The Ko Olina area hadn't changed much since the last time he'd driven down this street. Since it was mostly tourists and hotels, he didn't come to this area often. It looked safe, and he didn't feel bad about leaving Jenna here. She waved to him before she entered the parking lot of the Marriott. He pulled in behind her and then parked two cars over.

"I'm fine," Jenna said as she got out of her car.

"I know. I just like making sure."

She rolled her eyes and popped the trunk. He didn't give her a chance to grab the suitcase. He walked her in, standing back when she checked in at the front desk.

He'd never been inside any of these hotels, but he had been to the marina next door. Overall, Ko Olina was safe. He knew he could rest easy, knowing nothing would happen to Jenna here.

She turned to face him, her keycard in hand. "I'm checked in and going up."

"I can go up and make sure you get into your room safely."

She shook her head, but heat sizzled in her eyes. "It's not necessary. I'll be fine. They have good security here. Besides, this place is quiet."

Vine glanced around, then gave a sharp nod. "Okay. If anything seems amiss, call. I'm serious about that."

Her lips spread into a sweet smile, and she moved close, lifting up quickly and kissing his cheek. It had been a while since anyone had been that sweet to him. He wanted to pull her into his arms and kiss her lips until both of them were drunk on kisses and ready to do more. Then he would—Vine squelched the thought. He couldn't make a relationship with a CIA agent stationed in DC work. They would end badly because he'd be busy, and so would she.

"Okay, I'm going to go," Vine said.

"I'm headed up to bed. I'll see you in the morning."

Vine nodded and watched until she was in the elevator going up. He blew out a breath as he strolled out, wondering exactly how he would survive Jenna. She was smart, sexy, kind, sweet, intense, and she had a strong patriotic streak. She seemed perfect for him and, at the same time, exactly who he didn't need to go after.

Once back at his house, the guys started in on him. "I'm surprised you didn't ask her to sleep in your room," Astro said.

"Or stay with her," Wig added. "I mean, right now, you two could be in her room—"

"Shut up!" Vine bellowed. He didn't feel like putting up with their crap. Yes, he was attracted to Jenna, but it would never work out for them.

"I think you like her," Wig sang.

"Jesus, what are you, twelve?" Vine asked.

"Hey, Vine, we're just ribbing you. You want to dig deeper into Devlin?" Astro asked.

Vine reached up and grabbed the back of his

neck, letting out a long sigh. "I don't know. What do you guys think? Should we keep going on this? Are we barking up the wrong tree?"

"How about you call Tex?" Wig asked.

Vine let out a grumble that was full of aggravation and stress. "Do you really think it's time to get him involved? I mean, he's great. I just don't want to bug him if this is nothing."

"But if it is something, wouldn't it be better for him to know? Like maybe he can just go back and check what Jenna told us. He could confirm Jenna's story about what happened before. You know, what if the CIA was wrong about everything? What if Senator Devlin had nothing to do with the prior terrorist attack?"

Astro had a good point. It was time to involve Tex. Vine pulled out his phone and sent a quick note to their buddy, hoping Tex didn't think he was totally out in left field with some conspiracy theory absurdity.

Astro and Wig took off, promising to call him in the morning to see when he wanted to get together. Tex would be awake by the time he got up, and maybe they would have more information to go on.

Vine took a shower before stretching out in bed, trying to ignore the images of Jenna running through his mind. He rolled to his side and punched his pillow, then pulled it under his head as he thought about her smile, the way she flipped her hair when she was annoyed, and how good it felt to hear her laugh. With her near, he would have to keep his guard up. The last thing he wanted was for either of them to end up hurt. He just couldn't see a path forward for them. It was better to not have her at all than to experience her sweetness and have it ripped away.

The next morning the sun was up by the time he opened his eyes. The exhaustion of working hard for weeks had settled in his bones. He groaned and rolled over, carefully setting his feet on the floor as he tried to figure out what part of his body actually hurt and what part was just protesting overuse. He grabbed his phone to check messages on his way out of the bedroom. After he finished in the bathroom, he slid his thumb over his phone screen and saw he had a message from Tex.

The message said to call Tex. That could mean a lot. Vine grabbed a cup of coffee before settling at his table and tapping on Tex's number. It rang twice before the phone was answered.

"You have found yourself in the middle of a shit storm," Tex said.

"I have talent." Vine took a sip of his coffee, realizing whatever Jenna had told them had to be real. "Why don't you tell me how bad it is."

"I had to dig deeper than I ever have before. I'm not even sure I should know this stuff. That senator is dirtier than a sewer pipe. How did you get yourself into this mess?"

Vine swallowed his coffee and grunted. "During our last mission, we ended up being called into Turkey to do a favor for a friend of Admiral Light."

"You mean the Admiral Daniel Light? When I was in, Light was a captain. The man is a hard ass. How did that play out? I didn't think he had friends," Tex chuckled.

"You would've been delighted to see how this woman handled Light. The man was putty in her hands. Of course, he would kill me for saying that, but it was like they were father and daughter, almost."

Vine could hear Tex clicking away at the keyboard. He wondered what his buddy was looking up. He didn't have to wait long.

"Then you would be working with Jenna Mettler."

"I should stop being amazed when you find stuff

out like that. So did you know Senator Devlin was so dirty?"

"No. If I'd known he was this bad, I would've done something about it. I mean, I know politicians can be dirty, but this is bad. Just from the information you gave me, I see that he is the cause of those explosions that went off on that military base. I've looked at this before, but I never saw who was responsible. But now that I have the information connecting alias to alias and then to Devlin, I know now. I also found that the justice department stopped investigating him. He seems untouchable."

"I don't think I've ever heard you say someone was untouchable," Vine said.

Tex laughed. "I said seems, not is."

"I'd hate to be on the wrong end of the law when you're around."

"Yeah, but you're a goody-two-shoes. Even with everything you've done as a SEAL, you're squeaky clean."

Vine grunted as he sipped more coffee. "How can we help Jenna get the information she needs to bury Devlin?"

"I'm going to look into it today. I may not have an answer back to you today, so be careful. This guy would not even blink at killing you or your men.

And it could come off as a reasonable request through the proper channels. This jerk has access to everything and everyone. I'm not saying he could start a war, but he could start a battle that sends you and your team in and then change the playing field so you end up dead."

Vine blew out a breath. "Great, just what we need. The possibility of going into a dirty operation thinking it's clean."

"I'll call you if I find anything important. Stay safe and keep Jenna out of trouble. She is like a daughter to Admiral Light, and you don't want to be on his bad side either."

Vine ended the call and drank more coffee as he stared out the window at the fields below. This could easily go sideways. Maybe he and his men didn't need to be involved, but he had sworn an oath, and he would uphold his duty. The men and women who served in the military didn't deserve to be treated like trash, and the only way to keep them safe was to stop Senator Devlin.

CHAPTER 11

Jenna woke early and started investigating on her own long before coffee and breakfast were available. She'd wanted to sleep later, but her mind had been churning. When the sun lightened the sky enough she could see out her window, she headed out to find something to eat then drove over to Vine's house. Maybe she should've texted, but she figured he would be up.

When she knocked, she heard him grumbling inside then the door was jerked open. He blinked at her then waved her in.

"I didn't wake you, did I?" Jenna asked.

"No, but I'm feeling the effects of traveling. I need breakfast and more coffee."

"I should have picked up something for you on the way over."

"There's no reason for that. Besides, I usually eat too much to go out that often, especially for breakfast. Would you like anything?" Vine asked as he stepped into his kitchen.

"More coffee would be nice." Jenna followed him into the kitchen and found a mug, pouring herself some coffee before she moved to the kitchen table and settled with her computer open. "Sleep helped, but I'm not sure what to do next. I'm afraid there's no way to stop him. I can't find what we need."

Vine opened the refrigerator and pulled out a carton of eggs along with sausage and some vegetables. Jenna watched as he chopped the vegetables then turned on his stovetop. It had been a long while since she'd been with a guy who cooked breakfast. Usually, if she picked up someone for some fun, she either left before morning or kicked them out before they had a chance to get comfortable. It was odd being around a guy doing normal stuff. Her job was too dangerous to keep them close. It was one reason she was ready to leave the CIA. Life was passing her by, and being an agent was no longer fun.

"You look rather intense."

Jenna shrugged. "Everything I do is intense. My whole life is just one intense situation after another."

"I get that," Vine said as he flipped the eggs and grabbed a plate from the cabinet.

"When I first started, I enjoyed working for the CIA. Now I'm tired of it all. I guess I've just seen too much and done too much. I want to take a break and be myself."

Vine turned off the burner and brought his full plate over to the table. He sat down across from her, his expression guarded. She sipped her coffee and watched as he filled his fork, then let it hang in midair as he looked up and met her gaze.

"So you think you're done with the CIA?"

Jenna shrugged and sat back. "I've been doing this for a while. It seems like a good time to move on. I need a break. I know there will always be terrorists out there, and somebody needs to fight them. But I think it's time for that someone to be not me."

A knock sounded on his door, and Jenna jumped up. "I'll go get that while you eat."

Jenna moved quickly to the door. She pulled it open to find five guys, not just Robert and Forest.

"It looks like you picked up a few more," Jenna said. The guys filed in, introducing themselves as they went. There was Anthony, Ethan, and Jordan. They smiled, but underneath the veneer, she saw deadly men who moved with precision. She'd seen them in action in Turkey, and she knew what they were capable of.

"Did you all eat breakfast?" Jason called out from the kitchen.

"Sure did, boss. Quirk brought some fried rice, too," Forrest said.

"Which one of you is Quirk?" Jenna asked.

Jordan waved and flashed a big smile. "That would be me."

"Ah, that's an interesting nickname."

Jordan laughed as he carried a bag to the kitchen and set it on the counter, then pulled up a chair, flipping it around so he was straddling the back. "I'm used to it. Besides, it fits. It's not as bad as some of the nicknames I've heard over the years."

Jenna settled in her chair with her coffee and looked around the group. They seemed to get along with each other. She had wondered why Jason had so many kitchen chairs. Now it made sense. She also realized she was taking up one of the chairs.

Jenna moved to stand, but one of the guys put his hand on her shoulder. She turned to see Ethan beside her. "Don't move."

"But I'm taking up—"

Jason stood, his chair screeching on the floor. "One of them can stand. Really, they'll be fine. Besides, we're probably going to head into the den and talk there. I have some news." He picked up his plate and carried it to the sink.

"You have news? Why didn't you tell me about it?" Jenna asked.

Jason washed his plate with soap, rinsing the suds off then drying it before he turned and met her gaze. "I wanted to wait until the guys were here. Besides, I didn't want to have to tell it twice."

Jenna's chest tightened, and she could feel a yell rising. She swallowed it down, forcing herself to calm. He didn't work for her. They'd retrieved information she'd not been able to get. She needed to thank them, not yell. "Fine, I'm sure waiting didn't matter. So what is it?"

"You sure are impatient," Ethan said.

Jenna's jaw dropped as she stared at him. "You know what I do for a living, right?"

"Same, girl. But come on. We both have intense jobs," Ethan said as he sat back, looking like he was contemplating fishing in a pond, not taking down a terrorist.

"Give her a break, Minx. We're all impatient about this," Forrest said.

Ethan rolled his eyes. "You've got to chill out."

"Let's go into the den and get comfortable. I think today is going to be a long day." Jason led the way into the den where they could get a little more comfortable. The den was packed with three love seats. Just enough room for the crew to hang out.

A little guilt twisted through Jenna because she knew these guys were on a break, and yet, here they were helping her. She could do this on her own. She didn't need this group of SEALs to do her job. But she liked being with them. They were good people who gave her strength and made her feel good about the world again.

Her gaze strayed to Jason, and a shiver snaked through her. She glanced around, making sure no one noticed as they settled in the den. She moved fast and took a seat in one of the kitchen chairs they brought in, so she didn't end up sitting right beside Jason. The temptation would be too much. She tried to relax like Ethan had told her to, but her nerves were in high gear. Devlin was going to do something bad. She just hoped they stopped him before he did anything else to harm innocent people.

Jason cleared his throat before he started. "I put

in a call to Tex, and he's looking deeper into Devlin. He confirmed everything so far. He sent over some stuff, but not everything. He says this guy is as dirty as they come. He's going to dig deep and see what he can find out."

Jenna lifted her hand and held up one finger as she leaned forward. "Excuse me, but who is this Tex person? And what did he confirm?"

"He's about the best computer person in the world," Forrest said. "If you think I'm smart, he's a freaking genius."

Panic filled Jenna. "Can he be trusted?"

All the guys nodded. "I would trust him with everything," Jason said.

Jenna listened as the guys talked. She still felt a little panicked about them sharing the information with someone she didn't know. She guessed they had their own channels they worked through. Her heart still beat a little fast, and her stomach tightened. But they trusted this guy. She wasn't sure who she could trust after everything she had seen.

Maybe going into the CIA had been a mistake, but she'd never been given the option of working as a SEAL or in one of the other special forces units in the military. Her work life was built around distrust, and it seemed like the SEALs built relationships from trust. She guessed having to rely on the guy next to you to keep from dying built up the kind of belief in their teammates she'd never experienced. Watching them, it was like they were one beast broken into six parts. When she was put in the sandbox with another agent, they were like toddlers fighting over the one toy placed in front of them.

They spent another couple of hours digging, searching for more information about the senator. Around noon they took a break. The rest of the guys took off, heading out to grab food for lunch.

She had taken a moment to wash her face and freshen up in Jason's bathroom. Exhaustion pulled at her, but her work didn't rest even when she was tired.

Jenna stepped out of the bathroom and turned, running right into a solid wall of muscle. She glanced up, finding Jason in her way. His hand snaked around her back to keep her from falling over. His touch sent shivers down her spine. She wanted to lean in and kiss him.

"Sorry about that." Jenna tried to speak up, but only a whisper escaped her lips. He had this way of making her brain stop working. She could easily get lost in his touch, the sound of his voice, the way his gaze drilled into her and left her needing more. He made her feel crazy and alive. She wanted more but knew it was impossible.

Jason didn't say anything, instead, he lifted his other hand and ran his thumb over her cheek. A shiver raced down her spine as desire grew. Her breath hitched, and her head swam. She needed focus and clarity, but she really wanted this man.

"I should step away and not touch your soft skin," Jason said.

Jenna sank her teeth into her lower lip. His touch heated her to her core. She craved this. Her body responded with her nipples tightening. The thought of him touching her, kissing her, sliding his muscled torso against her body made her even hotter.

She didn't want him to walk away. Instead, she wanted to get closer to him. Her hand came up between them, and instead of pushing him away, she clenched his shirt in her fingers, holding him still. Her holding him was an illusion. A man his size and strength could easily get away from her, but he wasn't moving.

"You're right. We shouldn't touch." Jenna lifted her other hand and smoothed it down his arm, then reached around his back and pulled him closer.

"We both have jobs that will keep us separated. This isn't smart," Jason whispered.

Jenna shook her head and shuffled closer. She pressed her chest and then her pelvis against him, feeling his hard length against her belly. "No, it's not smart. I certainly shouldn't kiss you."

Outside, a car engine revved, and then doors slammed shut. The guys weren't quiet though she couldn't make out the words. Jenna sighed and stepped back, wiping her hand over her face. She looked up and met Jason's gaze. Sadness flashed in his depths. Her heart hurt for what they couldn't have. This wasn't the right time, though she wished it were. Maybe if everything worked out, and she was taken off Senator Devlin, she could explore whatever this was between them. For now, she would have to settle for just knowing him. Not that knowing he was in the world would ever be enough. She wanted it all, his touch, his kisses, his love, but maybe she wasn't built for love. Maybe seeing love at a distance was as good as she would ever get.

They worked until almost sundown, digging deep into every contact Devlin had. They were getting closer, but exhaustion held Jenna.

She stood and stretched, knowing she needed to take a break. Though she thought about staying at Jason's house, she knew she needed to go back to the hotel. Maybe if they had actually kissed, she would have asked if she could stretch out on his couch. But like everything else personal in her life, kissing Jason hadn't gone as planned.

"I'm going to head back to the hotel. I need some sleep," Jenna said.

"I'll follow you," Jason said.

"There's no reason. This is a safe area."

Disappointment played across his features. She

needed to step back now because she knew she would have to fly out tomorrow and head home to DC. She had to take action on everything they had learned. The rest of the guys stood and said they needed to go, too. They'd accomplished quite a bit, and she appreciated their work. They could have blown her off and gone about their lives, ignoring the trouble she'd found. Instead, they'd volunteered their time to help her.

"Thank you all for taking your days off and helping," Jenna said.

"Anything to make it safer for our military," Forrest said.

"I hope what we gathered will be enough to stop him." Jenna knew she had a tough road ahead in trying to stop Devlin from destroying peace and killing members of the military. There would have to be a lot of behind-the-scenes movement and coordination for this to be effective. They needed more information, but Devlin had hidden everything well. He wasn't sloppy. That much was evident.

Jason followed her to the door and held her back while the rest of the men left. They were alone. The air crackled between them. He didn't even have to touch her for her body to respond.

Jason leaned in so his lips were at her ear. "I don't

want you to go."

Jenna drew in a slow breath as Jason's words sank in. "I understand, but I shouldn't stay. We both have demanding jobs, and while I want to leave the CIA, it's going to be a while. It could be over a year before I'm able to disentangle myself from the demands placed on me."

"I don't mind waiting."

Jenna put her hand on his chest, which may have been a mistake. Desire pulled tight, but regret and disappointment wove through her. She wanted Jason, wanted to kiss every inch of his body, feel him pressing her into the mattress, but she couldn't give herself over yet.

"I hear what you're saying, but I don't want to grow attached to you, and if we go back inside and get naked, there's no way I won't be involved. And then if you figure out in six months that I'm not worth waiting for, I'd be devastated."

"I wouldn't do that."

She met his gaze and held it. "Then, in six months or a year when I'm free, I can come back. We can try then. If I'm worth waiting for, then getting together will be worth it in six months or a year."

Jason's lips thinned, and his eyes filled with desire. "I get why you're saying no. But I'm going to hold you to your promise to return. I'll hunt you down if you don't."

He reached for her and pulled her close, his lips sliding across hers in a gentle caress that left her breathless. His touch was molten lava, and her resolve to wait slipped. She couldn't fall into his arms because then nothing with Devlin would matter, and she knew she had to stop Devlin. Once she'd taken care of Devlin, she could think about Jason and his sweet kisses that tortured her dreams.

The kiss ended, and he stepped back. He crossed his arms over his chest and his gaze drilled into her. He wasn't playing fair, but she didn't mind. A part of her wished he would pull her into his arms and make love to her, showing her how much she would regret walking away. But he didn't, and she didn't push him back into the house to have her way with him. This was for the best.

Walking out to her car to drive to the hotel was one of the most difficult things she'd ever done. The sun was gone by the time she pulled into the parking lot and headed up to her room. The memory of Jason's kiss twisted through her mind, making her wish for more.

Once in her hotel room, she undressed and stepped into the shower, wishing Jason was with her.

All through her time in the CIA and even back to when she served in the military, she'd been able to keep her libido under control. But now she found she couldn't stop thinking of Jason. She wanted to feel him. She should go back to his house. She felt totally helpless against his draw.

Disgusted with her lack of self-control, she flipped off the water and stepped out of the shower, grabbing the towel and wrapping it around her body. She opened the door to the main room, letting the steam release. She should sit on the lanai and enjoy some of the hotel's ambiance because she would be leaving tomorrow.

She stepped out into the main room, and shock pulse through her. Her breath caught in her chest, and her movements seemed to stall. The wicked smile on Andrew's face made her stomach turn and her head pulse with pain. Her feet felt like she was trapped in peanut butter as she turned to run out the door.

She didn't make it. Pain exploded in her head right before she dropped to the ground. He rolled her to her back and stood over her. This could be the end of everything. She regretted not staying with Jason, regretted not making love to him. She only hoped he found peace after she was gone.

CHAPTER 13

Jason clenched his fists to keep from running out into the street as Jenna drove away. His heart ached like he'd been punched in the chest. Kissing Jenna had been better than he had guessed. Touching her felt amazing but kissing her had pulled deep down to the base of his soul, making him realize everything he had been missing out on.

Instead of wallowing in self-pity, Jason put on his running shoes and shorts and headed out for a long run. He needed to work out his issues and get his head on straight.

He had little doubt Jenna would be worth it. She was smart and sexy, perfect in every way. If he let her slip away, he knew he would regret it for the rest of his life. She was the woman he was supposed to be with. Everything about her made him come alive.

Unease had built and settled in his soul as the minutes ticked by. At first, he thought it was his legs aching from the run, but it wasn't that, nor was it his breathing. Something else was bugging him. He should have followed her to her hotel, but Ko Olina was a safe area. Still, something tugged at his mind and wouldn't let him go.

After his run, he did a workout of push-ups, squats and pull-ups in his garage as he tried to tick through the reasons he shouldn't go check in on her. She'd been in the military, and she was in the CIA. She knew how to take care of herself.

He showered then stood in front of his closet, debating about putting on street clothes versus dropping into his bed and sleeping off the weird feeling.

He pulled out his phone and sent Jenna a text. It had been a few hours, and maybe she was asleep, but maybe she would respond. After dropping to his mattress and trying to get comfortable for ten or so minutes, he got up and went to his closet. He tugged on shorts and a T-shirt before slipping on his socks and shoes. His pulse picked up as he acknowledged the prickly sensation twisting through his chest.

He was being ridiculous listening to his gut, but in battle, his gut didn't steer him wrong. His gut kept him alive time after time. He'd adjusted his stance, leaned down, dropped to a squat, all based on his gut feeling, and more than once, his gut had saved his life.

As he drove up the hill from his house to the main street, an image flashed in his mind. There'd been a car up here. He swore someone had been parked in the driveway of the house on the corner. But that house was empty, had been for eight months after the owner died. Their children didn't want to sell. So why had there been a car here? He didn't know the family, so one of them could have come to check on the house and he never would have known. But they lived in California and didn't come here often.

Unease increased as he thought about that car in the driveway. It seemed to take forever to get to the street with the hotels. On the way over, the few lights he encountered switched to red as he approached, stopping his flow. He waited as they went from red to green so slowly that he wondered if they were stuck. He'd considered turning across the light though it was red, but too many cars full of vacationers were around.

When he pulled up at the hotel, his heart nearly stopped. Two police cars and an ambulance sat in the lot. He should've been over here hours ago.

Vine stepped out of his car and moved to one of the officers. "What's going on?"

The officer sneered at first, then let his gaze travel up and down Vine's body before he nodded to the hotel lobby. "Some guy kidnapped a woman. He shot one of the dudes who tried to stop him."

Vine's throat closed up as he listened to the officer's words. "Any chance you have the name of the woman he kidnapped?"

The officer turned and narrowed his gaze. "You're military, correct?"

"I am. I have a friend staying here. She registered under the name Leanne Armstrong."

The officer looked at his notes then shook his head. "I'm sorry to say that was her."

Vine pulled out his phone as he turned away from the officer and dialed Tex.

"What's up?" Tex asked.

"Someone took her. The Marriott Ko Olina. Is there any way you can get the video? We need to know where he took her and what's going on."

Tex let out a low whistle as keys started to click on his end. While Tex typed away, Jason sent a note to his buddies. They were all probably asleep and knew they wouldn't be called out on a mission, so they may not even check their phones until morning.

Vine cursed himself for not following his gut. He should've known something bad was going on. If anything happened to Jenna, he wouldn't stop until he cut down Devlin and made sure the man didn't have the chance to so much as breathe again.

"It's going to take me a moment to get the information. Do you have any idea where he took her?" Tex asked.

"No clue. This is bad. I need to find out what's going on."

"I'll call you when I have any information. I'll send you the videos through email once I get them. Go home and regroup. We'll figure this out."

Vine ended the call, his anger almost out of control. Tears stung his eyes as he thought of how Devlin would torture Jenna. She wasn't safe. Nothing was safe. He should've listened to his gut and followed her. After this, he would never let her out of his sight again.

Jenna lay in a heap, her head pounded, and her mouth felt like someone had stuffed a dirty sock into it. Her wrists were bound with actual cuffs, not zip ties. She bounced as the floor beneath her fell away for a second. A noise filled the background. Where was she?

Jenna drew in a slow breath, trying to figure out the best way to escape as the ground bounced again then leveled off. Was she on a plane? She blinked, taking in the surroundings. She moved her head just a little. Tightly woven carpet scratched against her cheek. Industrial carpet on the floor. Now that she could think a little better, she could feel vibrations underneath her. The chairs were bolted into the floor. She glanced up, seeing the curved ceiling. Yep, she was in a plane, and based on the vibrations, they were in the air.

Someone stood and turned in the aisle in front of her. Their black shoes moved closer. It was a man based on the size of the shoes. She glanced up, spying Andrew. Her breath caught as memories flooded. She glanced down, seeing she was wearing a shirt and shorts. He'd also grabbed her flip-flops and shoved them on her feet.

Andrew dropped to a squat and leaned against the chair to his right. His lips spread into an evil grin. "Leanne, or should I say, Jenna, you should've left well enough alone."

She couldn't believe Andrew had flown to Hawaii to kidnap her. She guessed Devlin knew she was the agent and not Birch.

"Devlin wanted me to kill you, but I convinced him otherwise. I have plans for you. Don't worry, your little SEAL buddies will get theirs, too. They're going to pay for butting their noses in where they don't belong," Andrew said.

Jenna tugged at the cuffs on her wrists. They were tight, and she wouldn't be able to pull them loose. She was trapped, and there wasn't any way out. Devlin had her exactly where he wanted her, and there was nothing she could do. Maybe someone would eventually figure out what was going on, but it would be too late for her and probably too late for Jason's team.

Andrew pulled her up and led her to the bathroom. For a moment, she thought he would undo her hands. Instead, he pulled her shorts down and pushed her onto the toilet seat.

"I'm not stupid enough to undo your hands. You're just going to have to deal with this the way it is. You're lucky I'm not making you pee in your pants."

Jenna thought about head-butting him when he moved to pull her pants up, but what would she do then? They were trapped on this plane, and she had no way of getting out. If he'd used zip ties to bind her, she could break them. He must have known she could get free with those flimsy plastic strips.

After she finished in the bathroom, he undid the cuffs from behind her back and moved her hands to the front. She thought this was her lucky break until he shoved her into a seat that had been modified with a metal bar that locked and held her in place. There was no way she was getting out of this.

He left her alone after that, and she eventually fell asleep. When she woke, the plane was skipping down the runway. He'd closed all the window shades around her so she couldn't see where they were.

After the plane stopped rolling, Andrew moved to the back of the plane to collect her.

"Where are we?" Jenna asked.

Andrew chuckled and shook his head. "You'll find out soon enough where you are. But you're not going to like it." Andrew undid the bar holding her in place and jerked her up, pulling her close. "You can try to escape. I don't care. Not now."

"What does that mean?" Jenna asked.

"Well, Jenna, it means everyone outside that door is on my side and not yours. You can run out of here, but the minute you hit the tarmac, you're a target."

Her heart sped up. Dread slid through her as a shiver rocked her body. Where had he taken her? Andrew yanked her forward, dragging her down the aisle. No one on this plane would help her. Wherever she was, whatever she was walking into, would be terrible. She wouldn't make it out. She wished she had pushed to stay with Jason. Then again, Andrew might have broken into his house and killed him. Fear slid through her, taking her breath away. He was going to kill them, anyway. She prayed the SEALs were savvy enough to know they were in danger.

Andrew pushed her out of the plane and onto the first step. She blinked against the harsh light, trying to take in her surroundings. It took her a moment to realize four groups of men leaned against their vehicles, guns strapped to their chests. They had landed at a private airstrip, and from the looks of the vehicles and their surroundings, they were in Mexico. She was truly screwed. None of these men would help her. Instead, they would most likely sell her to the highest bidder.

CHAPTER 15

Vine's phone buzzed with a text message as he stepped into his house. He stared at the screen for half a second, wondering if this was a trap. They were on rest and shouldn't have been called up. But his team was specifically being asked for. It said so in the note.

Vine grabbed his bag and headed to base, knowing he would have to do a hell of a lot of convincing to get them to halt this mission. On the drive over, he received calls from both Forest and Wig. Neither one of them was happy.

Once on base, he stormed into the conference room and almost ran into Mustang, one of the other men who led a SEAL team.

"Whoa there. What's got you into a tear?"

Vine blew out a breath, trying to calm himself before he spoke. "We shouldn't have been called up. We just got back."

Mustang drew in a slow breath as he placed his hands on his hips, studying Vine. "Surely, there's a reason for it. They don't do this stuff without a good reason."

Vine closed his eyes for a second, knowing he had to slow down to explain this correctly. There was so much going on with Jenna and Devlin and all the stuff they'd found out. Now she was missing, kidnapped by some crazy jerk. He popped open his eyes and met Mustang's gaze. "You know when you get that feeling in your gut, and you know something is beyond wrong?"

Mustang's expression went serious. "Tell me more." Mustang had been a SEAL for longer than Vine, and he was a senior team lead. Vine was new to leading his own team. If Mustang was on their side, they might be able to influence the commander.

The door opened, and Midas, Pid, and Jag stepped in. Vine wished his guys were with him. He knew Astro could explain this better.

"Our last mission, we were pulled in to do a

special rescue of a senator. This is where it gets crazy."

"How crazy?" Jag asked.

"Like CIA is involved and investigating the senator crazy."

All three of the other guys raised their hands and stepped back. "Whoa, that's heavy," Mustang said.

The door opened, and the rest of Vine's team stepped inside. "What's heavy?" Minx asked.

Mustang leaned in, his eyes narrowing. "Does the rest of your team know about this?"

Vine nodded. "Yeah, they know. Tex knows about it, too."

Vine could tell that got Mustang's interest. The rest of the guys from Mustang's team leaned in, too. "So what did Tex say?"

Vine wiped his hand over his face as frustration built. "That Senator Devlin is dirty. Tex said he's the dirtiest he's ever seen. There's a reason we were called in, and it's not because there's a mission. I can almost guarantee Senator Devlin manufactured this to send us into a trap. Jenna was kidnapped."

"Wait, what? Who is Jenna?" Mustang asked.

"She's his girlfriend," Minx said.

"What does she have to do with the senator?" Pid asked.

"She's CIA. She is one of Devlin's aides. Really she's spying on him, and he doesn't know she's CIA. But I guess he does now since she was taken. There's evidence Devlin was behind the five hundred who died on that base in the Middle East."

"Shit," Mustang cursed as he reached up and squeezed his chin and pulled on his beard.

Vine knew convincing their superiors this was a set-up would be hard. They all knew about Tex and respected him, but they had orders they had to follow. If they were ordered to go in and fix a situation, they would have to have a really big reason to turn down that order.

"We're here to consult on this mission," Mustang said. "We've got your back. Have you called Tex to get him tracking your girlfriend?"

Vine shook his head. "Not yet."

"I'll get on that. You are all set up. This is going to be a bumpy ride," Mustang said.

Vine reached out and shook Mustang's hand, glad he had good men supporting him. It would take a heck of a lot to get out of this because he knew without a doubt, Devlin had manipulated this situation and would stop at nothing to get them off his tail.

When the meeting started, Vine thought he was going to have to disobey a direct command. He didn't want to be the type of SEAL that got a bad reputation for bucking authority, but there was no way this operation was on the up and up.

Mustang realized his distress and moved to the front of the room. "Commander Stewart, I know this is unusual, but the circumstances are very unusual."

Vine held his breath until Stewart nodded. "Continue. I want to hear where you're going with this, Mustang."

Mustang laid it out then asked Vine to throw in his concerns. It took them almost an hour to lay everything out, including the evidence Tex had procured.

They had new orders. Vine's team was going to head to the location they had been ordered to, knowing full well it was a trap. They would go in ready to attack, looking for the enemy as they landed. The Navy was also sending additional support, so they wouldn't be going in alone.

Mustang and his group were working with Tex to locate Jenna. They believed she was in a plane headed to Mexico.

Vine wanted to switch places with Mustang, but the commander would have none of that. If Senator Devlin was behind this and found out Vine was not headed to the location he expected, he might react rashly. It sucked heading into an assignment knowing it was dirty before they even left their base, but they were prepared. They had their mission, which wasn't what had been asked. Instead, they were looking for the tie-in to Devlin and how to get enough evidence to send him to jail.

Mustang and his team were set to take off right behind Vine's team. He met Mustang on the tarmac, his head vibrating with worry.

"I'll bring her home safe," Mustang said.

Vine nodded. "I know you will. I know you will do everything in your power to bring her home. But if they—"

"If they hurt her, they'll pay. I won't let you down," Mustang said.

Vine appreciated that Mustang didn't make him say it. He knew that if the kidnappers killed Jenna, Mustang would end their lives.

Leaving Hawaii and going in the opposite direction of Jenna nearly killed him. He would have his head in the game for his team, but the moment they finished, he was going to find Jenna and make sure she was okay. Senator Devlin would pay for this. There was no way in hell Vine would allow him to get away with kidnapping his almost girlfriend and threatening her life. That was a promise Vine intended to keep.

CHAPTER 16

Fear exploded through Jenna as she was pulled down the steps and loaded into one of the trucks. No one would ever find her now. Her only hope was an escape, but she doubted she would be left alone to work out any kind of getaway plan. These people were ruthless. They lived to bring pain to others and abuse them until they were all used up.

She had little doubt Vine would find out she had been captured. But he would never know where she'd been taken. Andrew and Senator Devlin would make sure he couldn't find her. She just prayed he and his team would escape whatever terrible plans Devlin had for them.

After about an hour, the vehicle stopped moving, and she was carried into a house and dropped unceremoniously onto the floor. Pain radiated down her leg and up her back, but she held in her reaction, not giving them the satisfaction of knowing she was in pain.

She scooted out of the center of the room and backed up against a wall. She pulled her legs close before wrapping her arms around them. She tried hard to blend into the background. She knew what type of place this was and knew she wouldn't escape unharmed.

Jenna used every skill she had in her arsenal to gather information. Find their weak points first. That was her mission. Her efforts seemed pointless. There were too many people here, too much activity. Someone would always be watching her every move.

An older woman came over and poked her with the end of a broom. She could see some of the men watching for her reaction. She had little doubt that if she fought back against this woman, they would punish her harshly for it.

When the woman asked for her to follow, Jenna stood and obeyed without any fight. These men were just looking for a reason to inflict pain. The older woman knew what the score was but was probably helpless against these men. Maybe she'd bought into their dogma. Or had she been forced into it? Jenna doubted this woman would be of any help.

Luckily Jenna understood enough Spanish to follow the woman's commands. The cuffs were removed, but they were in a room with bars on the window. The heavy door they had passed through had been locked behind her. Men with guns stood in the hall, just waiting for a chance to use them. She wouldn't escape this place without a good solid plan, and she didn't know enough to have a plan yet.

After she was allowed to shower and given a thin sundress, she was led to a table with food. She didn't realize how hungry she was until she sat down and took the first bite. She finished everything then follow the woman to what was basically a closet where she was told she would stay until they decided what to do with her. There was a bucket in the corner and a pitcher of water on a table. It wasn't the worst prison she'd ever seen the inside of, but it came close.

Now Jenna would wait and worry about Vine, wondering if he and his team would escape. Maybe one day in the future, if these men didn't beat her to death, she too would make it to freedom.

Mustang was on the phone with Tex as soon as their plane dropped low enough to pick up a signal. The men holding Jenna had driven from the landing strip and headed south. There were two compounds to the south where Tex believed she could be. They were landing close to the middle of nowhere, but somehow Tex had arranged transportation. They needed to go in and then get out quickly because, technically, they hadn't been authorized to go in.

"What is the plan, boss?" Jag asked.

"Go and get her and not get killed." Mustang didn't doubt they could retrieve Jenna quickly, but somebody was going to die, and he didn't want it to be them.

The plane landed, and they headed out, Aleck

driving as the rest of them made sure their equipment was ready. The sun sank lower in the sky, turning the few clouds orange and pink. Soon, it would be night. They would move in under cover of darkness, retrieve Jenna, and get out.

"We're almost to our location," Midas said.

"Good. We'll move as soon as the sun drops below the horizon," Mustang said. He had promised Vine he would bring Jenna home. He just hoped she was still alive when they got to her.

The sun dropped quickly after they parked behind a row of scrubby trees, and they headed out, moving rapidly over the near-desert terrain. Five guards walked the perimeter. Mustang had expected as much, but he knew this would start a gun battle if they didn't take out these guys quickly and efficiently.

"Jag and Slate, you two go down and take out the first two guards. Hide them well. We don't need any of the other guards figuring out their friends have gone down. Take out the others as you see fit."

"The idiot left their network open. I've got control of the cameras," Pid said.

"Good job. Do you have any idea where she is being held?" Mustang needed to know where to attack. The less time they spent in that compound, the better for them all.

"Give me a minute, and I'll see what I can find." Pid typed away at his computer, shaking his head before punching the air with his fist. "I found her. Back left corner, upstairs."

"I feel like climbing," Midas said.

"They have bars on the window," Pid added.

Midas rolled his shoulders and cracked his neck. "Well shit, I guess I have to go in through the door."

"Midas, Aleck, and Pid, you three come with me. We'll go in and get Jenna. Slate and Jag, you two keep us clear out here. Give us a heads up if it turns nasty."

"Sure thing," Jag said.

They had done rescues like this so many times before that they all knew what to do. This is what they lived for. Well, this and blowing shit up.

After Slate and Jag took out the first two guards, Mustang and his crew headed inside. Just past the door, Mustang ran into a guy and dropped him before he had a chance to signal anyone else in the house that they were being invaded. They moved with ease to the back left corner of the compound and headed upstairs, searching for Jenna. The two guards in the hall were harder to take out, but he and Aleck had them on the ground in seconds.

Mustang knew if Vine were here, he'd probably be freaking out. He remembered being out on that boat searching for Melody. He'd wanted to destroy everything in those moments he thought he couldn't find her. They opened door after door, finding women who weren't Jenna. After the tenth room, he worried the jerks had already taken Jenna somewhere else. He turned the hall and almost ran into a tall man dressed in a suit. He wasn't like the other guys guarding the house. This man was high up in the food chain.

The man in the suit screamed something, and Mustang knew it was going to be bad. He didn't have time to reason with the guy. Mustang lifted his gun, firing once. He didn't want to bring attention to them, but it was too late to pretend to be quiet.

"Looks like it's about to get crazy," Mustang said.

"We heard that out here," Slate said.

"Midas, find Jenna. The rest of us will clear the halls." Mustang was ready for this part of the mission and kind of relished it after seeing how many women were being held captive here.

"On it," Midas said as he started yanking doors open.

Mustang headed down to the end of the hall while Aleck moved back to the stairwell. Pid took the other hall and took out two men. These men had made their choices when they started peddling flesh instead of having honest jobs.

Too many minutes had passed, and Midas still hadn't found Jenna. Mustang worried they would never get her. Had she already been sold off? He knew Vine was the type of man who would search for Jenna until he found her. Mustang just prayed it didn't come to that.

CHAPTER 18

The plane landed on a small island off the coast of Papua New Guinea. They'd been called in to rescue a family held hostage by a terrorist group. It was hot, and rains had washed the road away. The situation was less than ideal. Add to the fact Vine figured this was a set-up, he wanted to abandon their mission but knew he had to follow through, or look like he was following through.

All of them were on high alert. They watched for unusual activity, looking for anything odd. Vine figured this was some type of ambush Devlin had sent them to.

"How far?" Astro asked.

"About two more clicks," Vine said.

Legs glanced around, his lips down in a frown. "This feels like an ambush."

"Eyes and ears," Vine said.

Each step brought more agitation and pressure. He hadn't heard if Mustang's team had rescued Jenna yet, and worry filled him. It sucked that one senator could cause so many problems just because he was dirty. As soon as they had Jenna back, Vine would make sure Devlin paid for his betrayal. The man had been serving in congress for a little over a decade, and in that time, he'd probably done more damage than anyone else Vine could think of.

Up ahead, Legs raised his right arm, signaling everyone should hold. His men moved as one unit as they breathed in and prepared for the worst.

Seconds ticked by then minutes. Vine was ready to tell them to move out when the first shot sounded. The branch next to his head exploded. He didn't have time to think. All he could do was react.

The men on his team were always ready to go in and destroy the enemy. When he'd become a SEAL, he hadn't guessed his most hated enemy would be someone he thought he could trust.

Vine took out one of the enemies, and Astro took out another. By the time the gunfire ended, all of his men were good, and they had four dead combatants on the ground.

"Do you think that's all?" Wig asked.

Vine shook his head. "No, I think it's only going to get worse. These guys look like hired mercenaries, not soldiers. Let's see what else they have for us."

Vine stayed with Wig, Astro, and Quirk while Legs and Minx circled around to the other side of the camp where the family was supposed to be. They moved slowly, looking for traps. He'd been in a lot of bad situations, gone through many battles, but this was the worst. He knew they were walking into a trap, but he just didn't know how bad it was. He doubted their intelligence because it had been supplied—by Devlin, he guessed—not gathered by their team.

His gut sensed something off. The tingle started low in his back and rose, making his head buzz. Danger was up ahead. He stopped Wig then told the rest of the guys to halt their movements over their comm system.

"What is it?" Quirk asked.

"I don't know. But something is wrong. I feel it in my guts," Vine said.

"I feel it, too," Astro said.

"Fall back, and let's regroup. Something is going on here that I don't like."

They moved back and met up about a mile away on the only hill in the area. Astro pulled out his scope and looked around, zeroing in on the camp.

"The guys in the camp seem upset," Astro said.

Vine grabbed his scope, finding the camp easily. A group of men in the camp were arguing. He guessed they thought the SEALs would keep coming, but he and his team had pulled back after sensing something wasn't right. If only he could hear what they were saying.

"What did they have planned for us?" Astro asked.

Vine watched a group of men head out from the camp in the direction he and Wig would've come in from. He was about to open his mouth and say something when an explosion rocked the area.

"Holy shit, they rigged the area with mines," Wig said.

Another explosion went off and then another. Vine blew out a harsh breath as anger rolled through him. "I think we can go in now. We need to find out what they know."

Cautiously his team approached the camp, searching for indications of landmines as they moved. When they entered the camp, the men reached for the guns but surrendered quickly once they experienced Vine's team in action. Four men were dead in front of them, and the rest realized they would die next.

It took Astro and Wig about thirty minutes to search their phones and find the request from Devlin. He had paid them ten thousand dollars to kill Vine and his team. Once they submitted proof the SEAL team was dead, the terrorists would receive another ten thousand dollars. It pissed off Vine that Senator Devlin thought his team was only worth twenty thousand dollars.

Vine called the information into command, asking them what they wanted him to do. It was a precarious situation. If they could tie it back to Devlin, then maybe they could take him down. But if they didn't prove Devlin was behind this, he could strike harder next time.

CHAPTER 19

Jenna had been pulled from the tiny room they'd shoved her into and followed some guy down one corridor then another, moving deeper into the compound and farther away from the room where they had told her to stay. She hated these men. Every step she took, she looked for a way to break free or kill them. Her best bet looked to be running. But with two men holding guns on her and all the men outside guarding the compound, she knew she wouldn't get far.

She was shoved into a room with a dimly lit stage. The door slammed behind her. She glanced around, blinking into the darkness, finally making out four men sitting around a table. One of them said something, and the others laughed.

She wanted to slink away but knew there was nowhere to run. She would end up being a toy for these men. She'd trained for situations like this. The only way to keep from going crazy was to blank her mind and just allow whatever was going to happen to happen.

She didn't want to give in and give up, but she had no weapons. She could maybe take down one of them, but she wouldn't get all four of them.

One of the men stood and moved toward her, his gaze filled with a predatory gleam. She felt like a defenseless mouse being stalked by an angry cat. Though she had no way of fighting back, that didn't mean she didn't look for opportunities. The guy wore a side holster that had a Glock locked in. She could go for his gun, but if she didn't take all four of them out quickly, she would be dead.

"Hello, señorita. Don't be so shy. Come and join us," the man said as he reached for her.

Jenna thought about ripping away from him, running to the far corner of the room and hiding. It wouldn't do any good. They would find her easily.

She walked beside the man, knowing if she resisted, they would only make it worse for her. She looked for a knife, anything to cause damage.

Nothing was lying around. She needed to grab his gun and kill him.

The men stood and moved to her. Their hands roved, touched, slipped under her dress, and took liberties she didn't offer. She hated the feel of their hands on her body. A shiver raced through her when of the guys ran his hands over her rear. His touch disgusted her. They would take and take until she was gone.

Jenna prepared to strike out when the sound of gunfire shocked them all into silence. None of the men were expecting a gun to go off, and they froze. She jumped back, getting free from their touch. She crept into the darkness, hiding behind a table as the men jumped into action and raced toward the door.

She breathed a sigh of relief since it seemed like they'd forgotten about her, leaving her alone in the room. Jenna couldn't believe her luck. They'd left her behind and left the door open.

She glanced around, searching for weapons. There were none. She slowly moved toward the door, her heart racing as she planned her escape. She didn't know what was going on, but she didn't intend to find out. She wanted to get away from these men and find some way home.

But her home wasn't safe, nowhere was safe for

her. Devlin had found her true identity. He would make her pay. She had to find a way to get back at him and eliminate the man.

Slowly, Jenna made her way down the halls, searching for an exit. She had to duck into the bathroom and hide, then she was forced to hide under a bed as men raced down the hall, heading toward the gunfire.

Jenna entered a room that had a door on the opposite side. She had no clue where she was in the house but knew she needed to get out. She moved to the door and was about to reach out and open it when it flew open. Her hand flew to her mouth to stop her scream as a big guy raced in behind one of the men from the room with the stage.

It took a second for Jenna to realize the second guy was an American soldier. When his gaze met hers, he flashed her a smile right before he took out another guy who had stepped into the room.

"Are you Jenna?"

She nodded, not believing her luck. How had this guy found her? "Vine, where is he?"

"Vine is my friend. We're going to get you out of here. Stay with me and do exactly what I say. My name is Pid."

"Thank you. Do you have an extra gun?" Jenna asked.

Pid's eyebrows shot up. "Do you know how to use it?"

"Oh yeah. I know how to use it. I'll watch your six."

"Okay, I'll give you my handgun. There are five other guys with me. Don't shoot any of us."

"Trust me, I won't."

Jenna followed the Navy SEAL down a set of twisting halls until they found a door to the outside. She was surprised when they didn't run into anyone else. They were about half a mile away when they met up with the other five SEALs. Relief never felt so good.

One of the men came over. "I'm Mustang. Are you hurt?"

Jenna shook her head. "No, just uncomfortable because I don't have shoes."

Mustang glanced down then met her gaze. "Can you walk?"

"As long as we don't have to walk over sharp shells or glass."

"If the pain gets too bad, one of us will carry you," Mustang said.

Jenna waved her hand and shook her head. "I'll make it. Let's go."

The path wasn't too bad, but by the time they made it to the vehicle, Jenna was glad she didn't have to walk anymore. Her feet had small cuts on the bottom. Luckily, they weren't deep. She sat between two of the guys and finally relaxed. The reality of the situation hit her. Tears ran down her cheeks as her body started to shiver.

The guy next to her gave her a blue bandanna. "It's all I have, but at least it's clean. My name is Midas."

Jenna wiped her eyes and blew her nose before turning to him. She gave him a wobbly smile. "Thank you, Midas. Thank you all for coming to save me."

"We'll be on a plane out of here in less than an hour," Mustang said.

"Where is Jason?" Jenna asked.

"He's on a mission," Midas said.

Fear blasted through Jenna, and she sat up straighter. "It's a trap." Would Jason know to watch for a double-cross? Would he understand he could be killed?

"He'll be fine. He knows what he's going into," Mustang said.

"As soon as you hear from Jason, I want to know." She'd never felt so lost as she did at that moment. She needed to make sure Jason didn't suffer because of her. She hated Devlin, despised him.

Mustang nodded as the vehicle took off. She stared out at the stark landscape.

"What will happen to those women back there?" Jenna asked.

"Most of the men are dead or in really bad shape. I guess they'll leave," Mustang said. Since this isn't an official mission and we were never in Mexico, I'm not sure. But at least they have a chance at freedom now."

She closed her eyes and rested her head against the seat. Devlin had put her in a terrible situation that could have ended up being something much worse.

The car stopped, and she realized she must've fallen asleep. She blinked open her eyes and spied a plane sitting on the runway. Relief filled her. She'd been saved. Now Jason's team just had to come home safe, too. If Jason or any of his men ended up dead, Jenna would throw caution to the wind and find a way to kill Devlin. There wasn't any way she would let him get away with this.

CHAPTER 20

Jenna woke as the plane bounced down the runway. She rubbed her eyes as she sat up, staring out the window, trying to make sense of where she was. It hadn't been long, so she knew they weren't in Hawaii. Out the window, it looked like a military base, not a commercial airport. And then there was water.

Jenna turned to Mustang, noting the intensity in his gaze. He was in work mode, serious and ready for action. "Where are we?" she asked.

"We had to make a stop for fuel," Mustang answered as he helped her stand. She hobbled after him. The pain in her feet wasn't too bad, but she needed to take care of the cuts and scrapes.

Aleck bent and picked her up, carrying her down

the metal stairs and out of the plane. She was grateful for their help. Once inside, she was allowed to shower and given clothes. A medic looked at her feet, patching her up and giving her some antibiotic ointment for the worst of the scrapes.

Once dressed, she was led to a conference room where she rejoined Mustang and his team. Sandwiches were brought in along with water and tea. She sat across from the guys, eating quietly as she processed everything that had happened.

She needed to contact her handler and tell them she was still alive, but she didn't want to give Devlin a heads up that she was okay. She didn't know how far the dirt had spread. What if someone in the CIA was working with Devlin?

She could go to DC and confront the jerk. She took another bite of food and swallowed as she thought about confronting Devlin. She would probably kill him, but not before he knew she'd survived.

He'd ordered a hit on her life. That hurt. She had to expose him and everything he'd done. It would be hard to get everything out in the open, but she would make people listen. Devlin needed to be in jail.

She swallowed the last of the sandwich, washing it down with tea as her mind turned to Jason. A lump formed in her throat. She closed her eyes, praying she would hear from him soon. She needed to know if he was dead or alive. Had the mission gotten the best of him and his team?

Devlin had gone to extreme measures. He had to be feeling the pinch to have ordered her killed. If she survived, he would have hell to pay. Maybe he thought of himself as untouchable.

"Have you heard from Jason?" Jenna blurted out, unable to stall the question any longer. Worry was taking over and starting to get the best of her. If anything happened to Jason, she would make sure Senator Devlin paid dearly.

No one said a word, and the pressure in her head built. She stayed in her chair as the men gathered at the other end of the room to discuss something. She should find out what was going on. She needed to know, but she feared they were discussing how to tell her Jason was dead.

She leaned forward, intent on resting her head on the table when a photo on the other side of the table caught her gaze. She narrowed her eyes, staring at what looked like wounded American soldiers. She stood and moved around the table, trying to get a better look. The photo was snatched out from in front of her.

Anger blasted through her, and she spun, ready for a fight. "What was that?"

Mustang slid the photo into a folder with other papers. "It's nothing."

"You're a bad liar. That was Jason, wasn't it? What happened to them? Is he dead?"

The guys who had rescued her stood around, their gazes falling everywhere but on her. Jenna felt like the air in her lungs had been scorched. The room started to spin. She clutched onto the chair beside her, fighting to stay upright.

"You're going to tell me what happened. Is Jason okay?"

The man who had been at the front of the room moved close, his lips a thin line. "I'm Commander Creed. This is hard to understand, but we need time."

Jenna's greatest fears blasted through her. Jason and his team had been killed. Her heart stilled as tears filled her eyes. She would stop at nothing to get back at Devlin. She would destroy everything for him. She wouldn't stop at ruining him politically. She would ruin everything for him. He had taken something precious, and now he had to pay.

"Jenna, it's not what you think," Mustang said.

"Then what is it?" Jenna screamed through her

tears. A wild feeling took over, and she wanted to punish Mustang and the rest of the men. But they hadn't done anything wrong. She gulped in air, trying to calm her sobs. She needed to get to Washington DC and kill Devlin as soon as possible. She would spend the rest of her life in prison, but it would be worth it.

Mustang waited for her to calm before he spoke. "Were trying to—"

"Don't tell her," Creed stated.

The lines in Mustang's forehead furrowed deeper as he shot Creed a harsh look. "She can be trusted."

"What are you saying?" Jenna asked.

"We have to keep this quiet," Mustang said.

Jenna stared from Mustang to Creed, her suspicions increasing. Were they trying to tell her the photo was fake? Was Jason alive? That photo had looked so real. As a CIA operative, she had photos like that faked. It was possible to do it. Still, seeing him dead in that photo had nearly stopped her heart and crushed her soul.

"What type of mission are Jason and his team on?" Jenna asked.

Mustang looked down at the ground then off in the distance. He didn't want to say, and that much was obvious. Finally, he met her stare. "We think we can take Devlin down."

Though he didn't answer the question, the pain in her heart grew less. "How? The Justice Department has already tried. Devlin is slippery."

"We have Andrew in our custody," Creed said.

Jenna felt like she'd been punched in the chest. "Does Devlin know?"

Mustang shook his head. "It's why we're here and not in Hawaii. We need to make sure no one sees you."

Fear blasted through her. "What about Jason's team?" Andrew being taken would lead to more repercussions against them, not less. Devlin would strike harder now.

"Can you trust me for a few more hours?" Mustang held her gaze, his honesty and integrity shining through.

Jenna's breath escaped in an explosive blast. She felt off balance. She needed to know if Jason was okay, but Mustang wouldn't give a straight answer. She had to read between the lines and figure it out. Mustang had said to trust him, and she guessed she would have to. Jason must still be alive. The photo said otherwise, but they'd so much as told her he was okay.

"Does Devlin know what happened in Mexico?" Jenna's voice sounded thin, raspy to her own ears. The emotions of thinking Jason was dead were getting to her.

Mustang shook his head. "No, we were able to keep that under wraps. He's in the dark for now. That's why we're trying to wrap up the other angle. If he thinks both of you are taken care of, he'll relax."

Jenna wanted a piece of this action, but she knew she couldn't do anything. Devlin believed her to be a prisoner in Mexico or maybe even dead by now. If she showed up in DC, it could destroy everything Mustang and his group were trying to do. She had to stay hidden and pray nothing bad had happened to Jason in the time it took to take Devlin down.

Would Jason come home just like Mustang had promised? If not, nothing would stop her from exacting revenge on Devlin.

CHAPTER 21

Vine didn't know if their plan had worked by the time they landed in Hawaii. He was pissed someone like Devlin existed in their government. He wanted to see Jenna and make sure she was okay, but she was still in California with Mustang's team. They'd saved her, bringing her home to safety. He would be grateful to all of them forever.

Finally, after a little bit of wrangling and pleading, he was allowed to phone her. The call connected, and he waited a beat, praying she really was fine. Mustang had sent word that she was okay, but he wouldn't believe it until he heard it from her lips.

"Hello," Jenna said.

Her voice was like music to his ears. Tears filled

his eyes, and he blew out a breath of relief. "Are you okay?" He needed to know everything was fine.

"I'm good, are you okay? Is everyone on your team okay?" Jenna asked.

Laughter bubbled up as relief filled him. "We're all good. Devlin meant to kill us, but he's not going to win."

It sounded like she was crying. His heart squeezed. This thing between them had built so fast. He didn't know why he felt the way he did. Attraction, love, whatever it was called, he had it. She filled his mind, danced through his thoughts, made him wish he could be with her all the time.

"How can we stop him?" Jenna asked.

Vine shook his head. "I don't know if it'll work. Mustang and Creed put a plan in place. If he takes the bait, he's going down. Hopefully, whatever power he has, he'll lose. He's been a blight on the US for far too long. This will all be over with at some point in the next day or so."

"I want to see you," Jenna said.

Vine sighed. "Same. I can't wait to hold you in my arms. I have to say, after this, I never want to let you go."

"I feel the same. I need to close things up in DC, but I don't want to be there anymore. I'm done."

Vine's stomach clenched. Could he ask Jenna to move in with him? Would she think it was too fast? So much had happened in such a short time. He felt like everything they'd experienced had driven them together.

"You're coming to Hawaii, right?" Vine wanted to punch himself. That wasn't the question he wanted to ask.

"I think so," Jenna said.

"I know this may seem odd, but I think you should stay with me." Vine held his breath, waiting for her to answer. If she didn't want to stay with him, he would understand. Or he would try to understand. He wanted her in his life and he wanted her in his house. Maybe it was crazy because they didn't know each other, but he needed her with him.

"If I overstay my welcome—"

Vine scoffed. "You won't overstay your welcome."

"But if I do, you'll tell me, right?"

Vine ducked his head, wishing they were having this conversation face to face. "I promise. But there's no way you will. I feel things with you that I've never felt before."

"I feel the same. I don't want to be without you. When I thought—" a sob escaped her lips, and Vine's heart stuttered.

"What did you think?"

Jenna sniffled then cleared her throat. "I saw that photo, and I thought your whole team…"

"Oh baby, I'm sorry you saw that. We were trying to convince Devlin we'd been killed."

"I hope it works because I want him to fry."

"Same, love. I feel the same."

Vine's throat grew thick with emotions. He wanted more time with Jenna to make sure they really were compatible. He felt things for her he had never felt before, and he knew this was it. She wasn't just some woman he wanted to screw. Jenna was everything to him. He could imagine waking up to her every morning. Spending his time off with her, loving her, just being with her.

"Mustang is telling me to wrap it up," Jenna said.

"I'll see you soon." Vine hated saying goodbye, but he had things he had to do, too.

The call ended, and Vine automatically wanted to call her back. But he still had things to do here on base. The team was staying on base just in case Senator Devlin had someone watching their houses. Jason wanted this to be over, but he wanted it to end in the right way. Devlin had to go down. If he didn't, then Jenna would never be safe again.

CHAPTER 22

Shortly after getting off the call with Jason, Jenna, along with Mustang's crew, hopped a plane and headed back to Hawaii. She was going home to Jason. She couldn't wait to see him.

The plane was a military transport, so there was no luxury at all. Jenna had flown worse working for the CIA, so she knew not to expect much and didn't care because she would be with Jason soon.

She prayed their strategy with Devlin worked. They needed him to go down hard. The worst part of this whole thing was she didn't know what would happen. Devlin was a thorn in her side, and she needed to get rid of him.

After reading a bit, listening to the guys shoot the bull, and staring off into space, she slept for a few hours. She woke when they landed in Hawaii and breathed out a sigh of relief. Now she could see Jason with her own two eyes.

Her muscles ached, and her feet were sore, but she was able to walk. She would walk all the way to Jason's house if she had to just to see him.

She'd expected to have to find a ride to his place, but when she stepped out of the plane and onto the runway, he was right there.

Jason ran to her and pulled her up into his arms, swinging her around. Pure joy filled her. When he set her down, she reached up and placed her hands on both sides of his face, staring up into his beautiful brown eyes. Her throat closed with emotions and tears gathered in her eyes.

"For a while there, I never thought I would see you again. I can't believe you're here," Jason said.

Tears ran down her cheeks as her emotions bubbled up. She pulled him close and pressed her lips to his. She never wanted to let him go. They could just stand here forever, and it wouldn't be long enough.

Someone cleared their throat, and they ended the kiss. Jenna took a step back so she didn't pull Jason into another kiss. She didn't know the man standing beside them, but Jason saluted him. She narrowed her gaze, looking at the stripes on his uniform. He was higher up in the ranks.

The man returned the salute before turning to her. "I'm Commander Stewart. I'm glad you're here. When these men told me what happened, I was a little skeptical. I've been working with naval intelligence for the last twenty-four hours, and we have enough to hopefully end his career."

Jenna reached out and shook his hand and flashed him a smile. "I hope so. This was not how I wanted my investigation with Devlin to go, but I'm glad it will be over. I never intended for anyone else to be drawn in. I'm just thankful none of your SEALs were injured or killed."

Commander Stewart chuckled. "It would take more than Devlin has to take out the SEALs. They are too tough for the likes of him."

"When will we know if the plan worked?" Jenna asked.

Stuart flashed her a smile. "It should be..." He looked at his watch and lifted his eyebrows. "About now."

Shock pulsed through her. "What do you mean about now?"

Stuart held out his arm, directing them inside. "Let's go watch. I'm sure CNN will have it playing."

Jenna wanted to ask questions, but she held them back, figuring Commander Stewart wasn't going to tell her anything unless he wanted to.

They stepped into a conference room where a big screen had the news on. Jason directed her to a chair. Before he sat down, he reached for something and handed it to her. It was her phone.

"How?"

"We got it from the police. I thought you would want it when you got back here."

Her heart swelled as he dropped into the seat beside her. They held hands as they watched the announcer on the TV say something about breaking for an important action that was taking place at the nation's capital. They all watched as the FBI and Homeland Security raided Senator Devlin's office. The news announcers didn't seem to know what was going on, but they knew it was big.

Jenna felt like a weight had been lifted from her shoulders. Devlin was led out in handcuffs. He was screaming and raving, but Jenna knew they had the evidence to lock him up. She didn't have to fear Devlin coming back to destroy her.

"What do you think?" Jason asked after Devlin was secured in the back of a car between two beefy FBI agents.

"That I'm free."

She still had to return to DC and end her career with the CIA. She needed a break. She couldn't spend the rest of her life going around chasing down other people. She wanted to live a normal life with Jason. Maybe they wouldn't last, and maybe nothing would work out, but she felt they had a chance at something good.

Her phone rang, and she turned it over, staring at the screen. It was her boss at the CIA. She had to deal with this now. Explaining everything to her boss took time. He wanted her back in DC. She agreed to a flight out late that evening.

She and Jason left the base and headed to his house. She was exhausted and was glad when he suggested a nap. When she woke, he wasn't in bed. Panic hit hard, and she jumped up then calmed as she realized she really was in Hawaii and was safe. After brushing her teeth, she wandered around his house and found Jason outside in the backyard tending to tomato plants.

"So you have a garden?" Jenna asked as she stepped outside. Jason stood and wiped his hands, knocking the dirt off. His lips twitched up in a smile that melted her heart. He moved closer, and she couldn't take her eyes off him. He was sexy in his shorts and T-shirt that fit so well she could see the ridge of his pecs.

"Do you feel rested?" Jason asked.

She nodded, and Jason's lips tilted up more. He reached out and pulled her close, covering her mouth with his. She opened for him, needing to drink him in.

He lifted the hem of her shirt, pulling the cloth off in one swift move. She let out a tiny shriek as she huddled closer to him, praying his neighbors couldn't see. She hadn't put on a bra, but then again, she hadn't expected Jason to strip her outside in his yard.

Jason ran his thumb over her cheek. "I'm on a curve, and no one is behind me. No one can see what we're doing."

Jenna looked around, seeing the thick hedge of bushes up against the fence surrounding his yard. He was right. No one could see them back here.

"That doesn't mean I want to do this out here," Jenna said.

His hand slid up her torso, and he caressed her breast, his thumb sliding over her nipple, increasing her desire. "We'll go inside today, but one night when it's dark out here, we're going to do this and more under the stars."

A shiver slid through her as desire built. She pressed her body harder against his. He held her close as he rocked his hips, showing her his desire.

"Before you leave for DC, I'm going to show you exactly how much I want you."

She bit her lower lip and stared up into his eyes. This man was everything she'd ever wanted. Jason brushed a quick kiss over her lips then stepped away. She didn't try to cover her breasts because only Jason could see her.

He led her inside to his bed, where he stripped off her clothes and pushed her to the mattress. His lips were on her ankles, then her knees and thighs. Finally, he kissed her hip, then moved over and slid his tongue up her slit, flicking her clit with an expertise she'd never experienced before.

She cried out as she arched up, trying to get closer to him. Her body vibrated with need as he licked and sucked. His mouth did things to her she'd never experienced. Her muscles clenched, and her toes curled as her feet arched. She couldn't get in enough air, and then it was like a rocket blasted off. Her heart pounded as she slammed her eyes closed.

She felt like she'd experienced heaven in his arms. He wasn't done, though. His fingers slid inside her pussy as he used his thumb to rub over her clit.

His lips kissed a lazy path up her torso to her breasts. His tongue swirled around her nipples, then he sucked down on one, leaving her gasping for breath.

After she'd had another orgasm, he rolled on a condom and slid into her. This was better than she had ever had it. Being with Jason, having him show her his love, was amazing.

He rocked in, his gaze holding hers as he lowered every few strokes for a kiss. The intensity in his eyes made her rethink everything. She wanted this man forever.

When he stilled above her, his mouth open and his eyes squeezed tight, she knew loving this man would always be easy. He'd made love to her like he knew her body. He'd given her exactly what she needed.

After he pulled out and rolled off her, he took care of the condom then stretched out beside her, holding her close. They stayed like that until late in the afternoon when she needed to leave for the airport. She didn't want to go, but she had to get her life settled before she came back here and started enjoying the next chapter in her life with Jason.

"You'll be safe, right?" Jason asked.

"Yes. Everything will be okay. I'll be safe and keep

an eye out. I won't be there long. I just need to do a few things and sign a few documents."

Jason kissed the tip of her nose before he stood and pulled her into the shower. He took his time washing her and bringing her to orgasm once more before he turned off the water. She didn't want to go, but it was time. When he drove her to the airport, she had tears in her eyes.

"This isn't goodbye. I'll see you in a few short weeks." Jason said.

"No, it isn't goodbye. I'll be back before you know it. Then we can start on the rest of our lives."

"I'll be here waiting for you."

Jenna went through security and glanced back, meeting his gaze. The love she felt for Jason had grown to the point she couldn't contain it. She wasn't sure how long this would take, but she would wrap everything up in DC and get back here as soon as possible because Jason was her future, and she was ready.

CHAPTER 23

Jenna finished at the CIA offices, handed in her credentials, and walked out a free woman. She had no ties, nothing binding her to DC or the mainland. All her banking, accounts, her personal business, everything could be done online.

Because of the amount of travel she'd done with the agency, she hadn't bought a house. She had a storage unit she needed to go through and a tiny apartment to clear out. All of her furniture would be donated, but the rest of her things would be shipped to Hawaii. She didn't have much, but she wanted to keep old family photographs and a few of her parents' items like old Christmas ornaments and other memorabilia.

Relief filled her as she made her way to the

storage unit. She was really free, and Devlin wouldn't bother her. The unit was on the outside of Arlington, Virginia, near Alexandria. She planned to go through boxes and throw away stuff she no longer wanted or needed, then head to her apartment. In two days, she had a company coming to take away her furniture. There wasn't anything she was attached to. Every piece she'd purchased had been for functionality, not because she felt attached to it.

At the storage unit, she began going through boxes, getting lost in old photographs of her family and friends. She missed her family, but not having anyone close had made being in the CIA easier. Once she was settled in Hawaii, she would send a note to Admiral Light. She figured he would want to know what she was up to.

She would need to rent space in a small container so she could ship her stuff to Hawaii. Once she cleaned out her apartment, she would have a better idea of what size she would need. She hoped this went fast because she really wanted to get back to Jason. She tried calling him, but he never answered. She guessed he was busy.

After a full day working in the storage unit, she headed home, picking up takeout on the way. She was happy everything had turned out well. Senator Devlin would be locked up for a long time. She would be able to live her life in peace. Maybe she would get a job at a shop or renting kayaks. She had enough money saved she could coast for a while, being picky about where she worked. She wouldn't want a desk job or something else where she would have to work when Jason was home. Security or police work was the last thing she wanted. She needed to be around happy people enjoying their lives.

When she pulled up in front of her apartment building, she stared at the rows of windows, thinking there really were just too many people packed into this area. She was glad to be moving to Hawaii, where the population was much lower. Even if Waikiki was full of tourists, out where Jason lived, life seemed peaceful and calm.

Jenna made her way upstairs to her apartment, exhausted from working so hard in the storage unit. She still had the keys in the door lock and the door halfway open when it hit her that something was wrong. She hadn't been expecting anything, so she hadn't looked for signs. Now it was too late. A hand reached out from behind the door and jerked her inside. They slammed the door, and shock pulse through her. Trapped, she searched for a weapon. She'd turned in her service revolver, and her own guns were stored in gun safes.

Jenna turned to see Devlin behind her, blood staining his shirt, his eyes black and blue. She took a step back, but he pulled out a gun, pointing it at her face.

Jenna froze, fear pelting her. Devlin had escaped and found her. She had no weapon, nothing on her, and she hadn't been vigilant. She had thought this was over. Deep down, she'd known it would never be over. Hope had her thinking Devlin would be locked away for good. She thought of Jason and how wonderful their life would've been. Now she would never know.

Vine hadn't even thought of taking time off. Then he went into work the next morning and asked his commander if he could have a few days. Their unit had been through a lot, and they weren't going anywhere. They needed time to regroup. He was given seven days and permission to travel to DC. He booked a flight leaving later that afternoon and began his trip to see Jenna. Maybe he should have told her he was coming to DC to see her, but he wanted to surprise her.

All the way over, he prayed she was still there when he arrived. Maybe he should've called, but he knew she would be happy he was there.

Tex had found out where she lived and had given Vine the information. It was late in the day by the time he finally arrived in DC, but he planned on going straight to her apartment. He would wait in the parking lot until she showed up if he had to.

Nerves hit hard as he made his way up to her apartment. He should've called. What if she had someone else? He didn't think she was involved with anyone else, but they didn't know each other well. He hoped she wasn't angry he showed up at her place without any warning.

He stood in front of her door, about ready to knock, when he heard someone yelling inside. Did she have a boyfriend? Was she breaking up with him? He didn't want to come between her and anyone else. She hadn't acted like there'd been someone else in her life, but he didn't know her. Maybe she'd been with another guy.

He was about to turn away when he heard glass crashing inside. If she was breaking up with someone, it wasn't going well. He had to help her. Even if this broke his heart, he needed to see what was going on.

Vine tried the door, finding it locked. His heart sank as defeat filled him. He should knock. As he raised his hand, he heard Jenna shrieking. He couldn't hold back.

Vine stepped back and tightened his muscles. He

lifted his leg and kicked hard. The door sprang open. He moved forward but froze. Devlin had a lamp lifted above Jenna's head.

His heart filled his throat and breathing became difficult. Kicking the door open had made them freeze for just a moment. He needed to get his act in gear, or he would lose Jenna.

There was blood all around her, and Jason feared he was too late. Anger mixed with panic.

Vine didn't have his gun, but as a SEAL, he knew he didn't need one. He lashed out and kicked Devlin, knocking him off Jenna. Devlin and the lamp fell, both of them crashing to the floor near Jenna.

Vine dove for the man, punching Devlin once and then again, then finally a third time, making sure Devlin was out cold before he turned to look at the love of his life.

His throat closed as thick emotions choked him up. He moved closer to her and searched for the wound creating so much blood. It was hard to breathe and harder to think as fear for Jenna skyrocketed.

Panic flooded Vine. He turned back, realizing he'd left Devlin unguarded and free to move around. He took the lamp cord and used it to bind Devlin's wrists before he turned to Jenna. She was still breathing, which gave him some hope.

A siren sounded in the parking lot, and then he heard someone running up the stairs. He checked Jenna, making sure she still had a pulse, before lifting his hands to his head and clasping his fingers behind his head.

The officer ran in, obviously prepared for a gunfight. Vine met his gaze, praying the guy didn't shoot.

"She needs an ambulance," Vine said.

"Shit. Is she dead?" the officer asked.

"No, she's alive."

It took about twenty, maybe thirty minutes, for everything to get sorted. In that time, the FBI showed up, and a commander in the Navy dropped by. Once the cop found out Devlin was the escaped prisoner most of DC was looking for, Vine was free to go. The naval officer drove him to the hospital and dropped him off, telling Vine to keep up with him so he knew what had gone on with Jenna.

Jenna's injuries weren't bad. Devlin's shot had gone wide, and she had a scrape on her arm that took out a chunk of skin and meat, but she would recover. The doctor stitched her up, but she was staying long enough to get a bag of fluid. The blood on her had been a mixture of Devlin's and hers, so she'd looked worse than she actually was.

Vine sat by her bed, drifting in and out of sleep as he waited for her to wake. He didn't know what time it was when she sat up and looked at him like she didn't know if any of this was real.

"You really are here?" Jenna asked.

Vine laughed and stood, moving to her bed. "I really am here. I have a few days of leave, and I wanted to spend it with you."

"What happened to Devlin?"

"He's back in prison," Jason said.

Jenna moaned and closed her eyes. "I'll never be free of him."

"I'll make sure you're safe," Vine said.

She opened her eyes and held his gaze. Her smile made his heart fill with pride. "I trust you, but I don't trust him at all. I tried to get his gun and shoot him. I meant to kill him."

"You hit his shoulder, so his injury is worse than yours."

Jenna laughed then moaned. "That hurts too much for just having a small wound."

He leaned down and kissed her forehead. "I'll take care of everything."

Jenna narrowed her gaze then shook her head. "I guess I'll just always be on the lookout for him."

Vine brushed his lips over hers this time. He wanted more time with her. When he returned home and she moved in, he would have a hard time going to work. "We'll find a way to be okay. Right now, you just need to heal."

"At least I went through everything in the storage unit. There isn't much work left. I'm ready to go back to Hawaii and leave this all behind."

Vine smiled down at her, his heart filling with love and pride. "I'll make sure everything is done."

He wasn't sure how he would do it, but somehow, he would find a way to make sure Jenna was safe. Devlin needed to be eliminated. If Vine had to, he would do the job himself to make sure Jenna could live in peace.

CHAPTER 25

Jenna woke in Jason's arms the first day back in Hawaii. She felt like her life was finally moving forward. They had spent a few wonderful days in DC, at first making sure all her furniture had been donated or sold, then packing up the last of her stuff before they played tourist the last two days. They got to know each other better, and she knew he was the one.

Jason blinked up at her, his smile wide. "Have you been awake for long?"

Jenna shook her head and stood, heading to the bathroom. "Not too long. Do you want coffee on the back patio?"

After she finished in the bathroom, she stepped out and smelled coffee brewing. Jason brushed past her as he headed to the bathroom and was cut before the coffee finished. He pulled her close, his lips finding hers in a quick kiss that left her breathless.

Jason ran his hands over her shoulders then up to cup her cheeks. "I love how you wake up ready to go in the morning. It's just another part I love about you."

Jenna's cheeks hurt from smiling so much. Every day with Jason was paradise. She figured they could be anywhere, and it would be wonderful. "Did you just say you love me?"

"I guess I did. I love you, Jenna Mettler."

She smiled up at him, knowing this was just the first of many magnificent days with the love of her life. "I love you, too, Jason Chase."

They stepped outside with their coffee and settled in the chairs, sipping as they watched the sun give light to the dawn. Jason had his phone out and was checking his emails when suddenly he gasped.

"What's wrong?" Jenna asked.

His eyebrows raised as he shook his head. "Nothing is wrong. But I think your troubles have been removed."

"What do you mean?"

"Someone took out Devlin in prison."

Jenna held her breath, not believing the news at first. "Took out as in killed?"

Jason nodded, excitement and happiness mixed in his expression. "He won't ever come back to kill you. He's gone. You're safe."

She let out a loud exhale as a shiver raced through her. "I feel bad being happy. Like it's wrong. But the man caused so many problems."

Jason took her hand and lifted it to his lips. "You don't have to feel bad. He was an evil man. He killed many and didn't deserve to live. We have proof he played a part in killing five hundred military men and women. You did your part, and now you're truly free."

Jenna held Jason's gaze then moved to kneel in front of him. "I didn't think I would ever be free. As long as he was around, I didn't know if I could tie myself to you. Not because I don't love you, but because I never want you to be hurt because of my previous job. Now everything is different."

Jason pulled her up and wrapped his arms around her waist, cupping the side of her face. "Marry me then."

Laughter bubbled up. "I was just about to ask you to marry me."

Jason's smile lit up his face. "Well, that's a yes for me."

"But first, I have to know," Jenna said.

Jason grew serious. "Know what?"

"Your name, how did you get the name Vine?"

Jason rolled his eyes and let his head drop back. "It's so embarrassing."

"Tell me."

He blew out a breath and shook his head. "We were out in the wilderness of Michigan and I ended up with poison ivy on my dick and balls and my ass."

"What?"

"It was a training mission. I should have known better. I needed something to wipe with."

"Wait, so they call you Vine because you got poison ivy on your butt, and other junk?"

"Oh yeah. It was bad. I was in the infirmary for three days. I was young, just seventeen and didn't know. I'd been a city boy, and no one had ever told me plants could make you blister like nobody's business."

She wanted to be able to laugh at his nickname, but there was no way she could laugh at his story. "That sucks."

"On the upside, I can identify every plant that makes you blister in existence. I also took an interest in botany and know what plants we can eat when we go out on missions. It has been helpful."

She leaned in and kissed him, drinking in his sweetness as her heart twisted for him. "I guess we're getting married."

Jason's eyes twinkled with happiness. "I guess we are."

She'd done it, found someone to love and live with. She'd never thought she would really have anyone. This man was her soul mate, the one who meant the world.

Jenna's life looked totally different than it had when she first met Jason. No longer a CIA operative, she would live a quiet life and was ready for whatever Jason brought to their relationship. She had the man of her dreams, and now she was ready to live out those dreams with the best man she'd ever known.

The End

To read more books like Jenna's SEAL, read *A SEAL for Candace* by Julia Bright.

Finding Home

Jenna's SEAL

Fighting for Home

A SEAL for Candace

A SEAL for Deb

A SEAL for Elise

A SEAL for Trixie

A SEAL for Raven

Special Forces: Operation Alpha

Saving Lorelei

Rescuing Amy

Saving Sloan

Seeking Justice

Justice for Amber

Searching for Keeley

Justice for Oswin

Safety for Eve

Dark Eagle Series

Survive The Fall

Live Past The Edge

Hold on Through the Pain

Endure the Darkness

Storm Corp Series

Determined

Standalone Romance

Acting The Part

All Business

Just One Taste

ABOUT THE AUTHOR

Julia Bright is the author of the contemporary military romance Dark Eagle series and is an Operation Alpha Author. Julia lives in the south where "bless your heart" is an insult and "shut up" shows love. Julia has been reading since they could open a book and has taken the passion for words and combined it with the love of travel to create stories full of passion and excitement. If you love a good book with a fantastic happily ever after, you'll enjoy a Julia Bright novel. For a dash of paranormal romance and urban fantasy, pick up a book from Julia's USA Today Bestselling JS Bright pen name

facebook.com/AuthorJuliaBright

amazon.com/Julia-Bright/e

bookbub.com/authors/julia-bright

There are many more books in this fan fiction world than listed here, for an up-to-date list go to www.AcesPress.com

You can also visit our Amazon page at:
http://www.amazon.com/author/operationalpha

Special Forces: Operation Alpha World
Christie Adams: Charity's Heart
Denise Agnew: Dangerous to Hold
Shauna Allen: Awakening Aubrey
Brynne Asher: Blackburn
Linzi Baxter: Unlocking Dreams
Jennifer Becker: Hiding Catherine
Alice Bello: Shadowing Milly
Heather Blair: Rescue Me
Misha Blake: Flash
Anna Blakely: Rescuing Gracelynn
Julia Bright: Saving Lorelei
Cara Carnes: Protecting Mari
Kendra Mei Chailyn: Beast
Melissa Kay Clarke: Rescuing Annabeth
Samantha A. Cole: Handling Haven
Sue Coletta: Hacked
Melissa Combs: Gallant
Lorelei Confer: Protecting Sara

Anne Conley: Redemption for Misty

KaLyn Cooper: Rescuing Melina

Janie Crouch: Storm

Liz Crowe: Marking Mariah

Sarah Curtis: Securing the Odds

Jordan Dane: Redemption for Avery

Tarina Deaton: Found in the Lost

Aspen Drake, Intense

KL Donn: Unraveling Love

Riley Edwards: Protecting Olivia

PJ Fiala: Defending Sophie

Nicole Flockton: Protecting Maria

Alexa Gregory: Backdraft

Michele Gwynn: Rescuing Emma

Casey Hagen: Shielding Nebraska

Desiree Holt: Protecting Maddie

Kathy Ivan: Saving Sarah

Kris Jacen, Be With Me

Jesse Jacobson: Protecting Honor

Silver James: Rescue Moon

Becca Jameson: Saving Sofia

Kate Kinsley: Protecting Ava

Rayne Lewis: Justice for Mary

Heather Long: Securing Arizona

Gennita Low: No Protection

Kirsten Lynn: Joining Forces for Jesse

Margaret Madigan: Bang for the Buck

Trish McCallan: Hero Under Fire

Kimberly McGath: The Predecessor

Rachel McNeely: The SEAL's Surprise Baby

KD Michaels: Saving Laura

Lynn Michaels: Rescuing Kyle

Olivia Michaels: Protecting Harper

Wren Michaels: The Fox & The Hound

Annie Miller: Securing Willow

Kat Mizera: Protecting Bobbi

Keira Montclair, Wolf and the Wild Scots

Mary B Moore: Force Protection

LeTeisha Newton: Protecting Butterfly

Angela Nicole: Protecting the Donna

MJ Nightingale: Protecting Beauty

Sarah O'Rourke: Saving Liberty

Victoria Paige: Reclaiming Izabel

Anne L. Parks: Mason

Debra Parmley: Protecting Pippa

Lainey Reese: Protecting New York

KeKe Renée: Protecting Bria

TL Reeve and Michele Ryan: Extracting Mateo

Elena M. Reyes: Keeping Ava

Deanna L. Rowley: Saving Veronica

Angela Rush: Charlotte

Rose Smith: Saving Satin

Jenika Snow: Protecting Lily

Lynne St. James: SEAL's Spitfire

Dee Stewart: Conner

Harley Stone: Rescuing Mercy

Sarah Stone: Shielding Grace

Jen Talty: Burning Desire

Reina Torres, Rescuing Hi'ilani

Savvi V: Loving Lex

Megan Vernon: Protecting Us

LJ Vickery: Circus Comes to Town

Rachel Young: Because of Marissa

R. C. Wynne: Shadows Renewed

Delta Team Three Series
Lori Ryan: Nori's Delta

Becca Jameson: Destiny's Delta

Lynne St James, Gwen's Delta

Elle James: Ivy's Delta

Riley Edwards: Hope's Delta

Police and Fire: Operation Alpha World
Freya Barker: Burning for Autumn

B.P. Beth: Scott

Jane Blythe: Salvaging Marigold

Julia Bright, Justice for Amber

Anna Brooks, Guarding Georgia

KaLyn Cooper: Justice for Gwen
Aspen Drake: Sheltering Emma
Emily Gray: Shelter for Allegra
Alexa Gregory: Backdraft
Deanndra Hall: Shelter for Sharla
Barb Han: Kace
EM Hayes: Gambling for Ashleigh
India Kells: Shadow Killer
CM Steele: Guarding Hope
Reina Torres: Justice for Sloane
Aubree Valentine, Justice for Danielle
Maddie Wade: Finding English
Stacey Wilk: Stage Fright
Laine Vess: Justice for Lauren

Tarpley VFD Series
Silver James, Fighting for Elena
Deanndra Hall, Fighting for Carly
Haven Rose, Fighting for Calliope
MJ Nightingale, Fighting for Jemma
TL Reeve, Fighting for Brittney
Nicole Flockton, Fighting for Nadia

As you know, this book included at least one character from Susan Stoker's books. To check out more, see below.

SEAL Team Hawaii Series

Finding Elodie

Finding Lexie

Finding Kenna (Oct 2021)

Finding Monica (May 2022)

Finding Carly (TBA)

Finding Ashlyn (TBA)

Finding Jodelle (TBA)

Eagle Point Search & Rescue

Searching for Lilly (Mar 2022)

Searching for Elsie (Jun 2022)

Searching for Bristol (Nov 2022)

Searching for Caryn (TBA)

Searching for Finley (TBA)

Searching for Heather (TBA)

Searching for Khloe (TBA)

The Refuge Series

Deserving Alaska (Aug 2022)

Deserving Henley (Jan 2023)

Deserving Reese (TBA)

Deserving Cora (TBA)

Deserving Lara (TBA)

Deserving Maisy (TBA)

Deserving Ryleigh (TBA)

Delta Team Two Series

Shielding Gillian

Shielding Kinley

Shielding Aspen

Shielding Jayme (novella)

Shielding Riley

Shielding Devyn

Shielding Ember

Shielding Sierra (Jan 2022)

SEAL of Protection: Legacy Series

Securing Caite (FREE!)

Securing Brenae (novella)

Securing Sidney

Securing Piper

Securing Zoey

Securing Avery

Securing Kalee

Securing Jane

Delta Force Heroes Series

Rescuing Rayne (FREE!)
Rescuing Aimee (novella)
Rescuing Emily
Rescuing Harley
Marrying Emily (novella)
Rescuing Kassie
Rescuing Bryn
Rescuing Casey
Rescuing Sadie (novella)
Rescuing Wendy
Rescuing Mary
Rescuing Macie (novella)
Rescuing Annie (Feb 2022)

Badge of Honor: Texas Heroes Series

Justice for Mackenzie (FREE!)
Justice for Mickie
Justice for Corrie
Justice for Laine (novella)
Shelter for Elizabeth
Justice for Boone
Shelter for Adeline
Shelter for Sophie
Justice for Erin
Justice for Milena

Shelter for Blythe
Justice for Hope
Shelter for Quinn
Shelter for Koren
Shelter for Penelope

SEAL of Protection Series

Protecting Caroline (FREE!)
Protecting Alabama
Protecting Fiona
Marrying Caroline (novella)
Protecting Summer
Protecting Cheyenne
Protecting Jessyka
Protecting Julie (novella)
Protecting Melody
Protecting the Future
Protecting Kiera (novella)
Protecting Alabama's Kids (novella)
Protecting Dakota

New York Times, USA Today and *Wall Street Journal* Bestselling Author Susan Stoker has a heart as big as the state of Tennessee where she lives, but this all American girl has also spent the last fourteen years living in Missouri, California, Colorado, Indiana, and Texas. She's married to a retired Army man who now gets to follow *her* around the country.

www.stokeraces.com
www.AcesPress.com
susan@stokeraces.com

207

Made in United States
Orlando, FL
12 May 2024